"Welcome and wassail, friends and neighbors. . . . I have invited you here this day for two reasons. One is an occasion of celebration, the other to see justice done." Silence settled over the crowd. "On this day I announce the marriage of my daughter, Lida, to Icenius of Brittania."

Lida said nothing; she was stunned.

"The other is to see a spy punished. Bring in the dog," he roared. The doors to the Hall opened and Casca was kicked and dragged into the center of the room.

Pointing a dirty finger at the Roman, Ragnar proclaimed, "This dog here, who has eaten at my table and claimed the laws of hospitality, is a spy for Rome. . . . I sentence you, spy of Rome, to the tide stakes!"

CASCA:

THE BARBARIAN

BARRY SADLER

CHARTER
NEW YORK

A Division of Charter Communications Inc.
A GROSSET & DUNLAP COMPANY
51 Madison Avenue
New York, New York 10010

My name is Doctor Julius Goldman.

For some years now I have been involved with the fate of a man known only to a few and believed by the majority of those to be no more than a myth from the distant past. Yes! a myth . . . like the hero of the Epics of Gilgamesh or the Kulkulkan of the Mayan legends, and even the story of the wandering Jew. The man I know came to me with a wound that should have been fatal, but *he* did not die. From that first meeting our lives have been intertwined.

For some reason, he has a compulsion to finish the story of his life. A story that for me began in the hospital at Nha Trang, in South Vietnam, over ten years ago. From time to time we have met, and each time a force comes over me, as it did in that hospital. I am drawn again into the past of the man I first knew as Sergeant Casey Romain—a man who the rest of the world only knows dimly . . . as the man who killed Jesus on Golgatha.

He is the Roman legionnaire, Casca Rufio Longinus.

And, as Casca has his compulsion to finish what he began with me, I have the same drive to put down his story. I know most won't believe me, but then, that doesn't really matter; *I* know it's *real*, and even today . . .

Casca lives to walk the earth until the Second Coming . . .
Casca Lives!

Prologue

Stinging sand whipped at his eyes as the wind howled about him, trying to blow his robes free to sail over the desert with the sandstorm. His horse whinnied and shied away from the wind, trying to turn around and put its rear to the cutting bits of grit.

Casca finally agreed and took shelter on the leeward side of a dune. Tying his horse to a bush, he pulled his robe over his head and sat with his back to the wind. Feeling the sand slowly begin to pile up against him, he kept his head down and pulled his precious goatskin of water closer between his legs. There was nothing to do now but wait. His horse whinnied again. The beast didn't like this region of whirling, biting sand devils and screaming winds. As far as that went, the horse didn't particularly like his new master. The man didn't have the smell of those who had owned him before. But Casca really didn't give a damn whether the horse liked him or not. As far as he was concerned, he would rather eat one of the damn things than ride it, and if he didn't come across some food soon, that would probably not be far in the future. The horse's previous master was beyond any complaint.

The Arab's body lay two days behind, the sun and wind drying it into another of the thousands of shriveled, desiccated husks of humanity that littered the floor of the Persian desert. The former member of the victorious legions of Avidius Cassius felt no remorse. If the bastard hadn't thought Casca was easy picking, he wouldn't be lying back there with the large blue flies trying to suck out the last remaining bits of moisture from his body.

A sand lizard, blown from its shelter under the dune, crawled between his legs and sat looking up at him. Casca smiled through cracked lips. "Welcome, little friend, to what protection I can give. We'll just have to wait this thing out, and if you don't bite, neither will I."

Back on the battlefield of Ctesiphon were forty thousand that would never bite or do anything else again. He had no sense of guilt for deserting the Eagle standards of Rome. Avidius Cassius had promised the warriors of Parthia that he would spare the city and its people if they came out to do battle, but even now Casca knew that thousands were on their way to the slave pens of Syria and that the city was still burning. It took a long time for a city to die—much longer than it did for a man.

He had had enough of slaughter and wanted no more than to get away to some place where the stench of death didn't fill the nostrils. But even that was to be denied him. If that stupid Arab hadn't tried to take him on, the man would still be living, feeling the blood course through his veins and the beat of his heart.

The sand had reached up to his waist and began

to flow around him; he knew that if it didn't stop soon he would be buried. He wondered how his horse was faring—for some time now he had heard nothing save the keening of the wind over the dunes.

He pulled the stopper from the goatskin and took a pull of the strong-tasting, brackish water. The lizard watched him, its eyes moving independently from one another; it missed nothing. Casca ran his tongue over his lips, put his hand down in front of the small creature, and poured a couple of drops into his palm, holding it still. The lizard twitched its tail, looking as if it were thinking about running, then, making up its mind, moved onto the man's palm and drank, its mouth opening and closing like a fish trying to breathe air. Then, finishing quick as a blink, it flashed back to its place between Casca's legs.

Casca wiped the remaining damp spot across his lips. The heat of the sand on his back was drugging him, making his eyes feel heavy and gritty. He sighed and pulled his robe closer about him. Looking at his guest, he spoke, eyes red rimmed and dull from heat ard fatigue.

"Well, little friend, I'm going to crap out for a while. You keep watch for me and I'll see you later." His eyes closed and the darkness set in—the kind that eats up the hours and rests the soul. He slept, not knowing when the storm passed by and the night sky shone clear and stark in its brilliance, the stars each set perfect in the firmament of the heavens.

Some time during the storm the horse broke free and followed the course of the wind.

The silence woke him. Slowly, stiff-jointed, he

moved. The sand, which had built up to his shoulders, slid off in slow waves. The lizard blinked once, twice at the disturbance, and was gone, burrowing back into the shelter of the dunes to wait for the warmth of the next dawn to start the blood flowing through its veins. Casca wished him well.

Rising, he looked for his horse, which he knew was long gone. Well, he thought, that's about normal. If it wasn't for bad luck, I wouldn't have any. He pulled his burnoose closer about him. The insulating sand had kept him warm, but now the night chill of the desert made itself known. It always amazed him, the contrast between the burning sun and heat of the day, which could kill a man without water in six hours, and the chill of the night. He climbed the nearest dune and looked out over the open expanse, ghostly lit by the clear night sky. There was nothing, not even the howl of a desert jackal; it was empty. He had hoped perhaps to see his horse, but knew there was little or no chance. Sighing, he went back down the slope. Sliding and kneeling, he dug himself a small pit in the sand and lay down, pulling the sand back around him to serve as a blanket to keep the worst of the cold out. He closed his eyes again and slept in the small, shallow grave.

Just minutes before dawn, Casca pulled himself out of his cocoon and rose, stretching his arms to the sky. He straightened, cracking the sore bones in his back and neck. He took a deep breath and exhaled. Moving to the bush where he had tied his horse, he dug in the sand and pulled out his pack, searching the meager content. Finding out a small, hard, rancid horse curd and a chunk of ten-day-old bread, he climbed back up the crest of the dune to await the coming of the sun.

Taking another small swig of tepid water to wet his throat before attempting to eat the rock-hard and rancid curds, he hunched down in the sand, waiting, his eyes toward the East. The thin, pre-dawn glow lay on the horizon. The sun would be rising soon, and with it would come the brain-cooking heat of the desert.

He put the taste of the food out of his mind and concentrated on chewing the hard bread. Eating slowly, he would let each bite soften and turn sweet in his mouth before swallowing. Careful of how much he ate, he saved most of the curds for later, knowing he would need the strength they could give him then. A light breeze was beginning to pick up with the coming of the sun, as it usually did in the desert. There was no trace of moisture in the air. He was still a long way from the ocean, and the waters of the Tigris and Euphrates lay far behind him.

Before the storm had hit, he had been staying fairly close to the same route he and the legions of Gaius Avidius Cassius had taken in their invasion of Parthia when they had left their staging area at Damascus. It was one thing to cross the desert as part of a great army with supplies laid in along the way, and quite another to try it in reverse, alone and without any stores of food or water to make it across the five hundred miles back. It would be stupid to have tried to make his way along the Euphrates or Tigris. He would have been sure to have run into patrols from the Gelions that had taken Amida and Europa, and he had no desire to have his carcass strung up and crucified for desertion.

The sun was up now, a massive red-gold orb slowly rising. He could see how the Greeks in the legends called it "the fiery chariot of Apollo." In these lands, the sun was everything—the giver of life, and the taker. The ground he would have to cover was bad enough, but to the south was the monstrous ocean of sands that the wandering Semite tribes of Arabia fought so fiercely to keep under control. As far as he was concerned, they could keep it all.

Casca rose from the sands and wiped the scanty remnants of his morning meal from his fingertips and face. The curds had left a sour taste in his mouth, but he resisted the temptation to wash it away with another drink of his scant supply of water. The advance of the sun was beginning to drive the chill of the night from his bones. He knew the day would be a bitch, so he had to try to find some shade before the worst of the heat came. He could see from his position on top of the dune a distant line of mountains to the northwest. They were delicate shades of rose and pink now, but with the rising of the day they would change into shimmering, distant, gray crags of barren rock, cracked and split into schisms from the endless heating and cooling of the centuries.

That was where he must go if water and food were to be found. What there was would be found in those inhospitable stones. He gathered his possessions and made them into a pack, using a couple of strips torn from his robe to sling them over his shoulder.

The soldier of Rome walked out onto the shifting floor of the desert. With every step the sand worked its way into his sandals and then spilled out again into thin streams. He settled down into the mile-eating, steady tread of the professional foot soldier, the sun on his back pushing him on.

He walked slowly but steadily, avoiding the desire to rush, knowing that that would use him up faster than his measured pace. He would have to make the mountains by the next day or run out of water. Even now the base of the crags could not be seen. The top half was floating over the floor, the desert shifting and riding on shimmering heat waves. The day found him crossing a field of stones with lizards and serpents watching his progress. His step was already slowing down, the heat a constant drain, drawing off his life's essence and strength. The water bag at his side sloshed continuously, tempting him to raise it to his mouth and drink, or wash his face to get rid of the caked-up dust and sweat and streaked grit around the corners of his eyes.

Stopping, he raised his head and looked out across the field of stones and serpents. He had to stop and wait out the worst of the heat. A single, darker object rose from the rocky floor. It was a large boulder that hadn't yet given into time's remorseless efforts to wear it down to the size of its neighbors. It stood like a lonely sentinel, guarding nothing.

Casca sat down on the shaded side of the stone. It was about as tall as he was and five feet around, but it also had the only shade for miles. He scraped away the surface layer of rocks, knowing they would be the hottest. Sitting on them would have drawn some of his moisture. He pulled his robes over him, forming a tent, and leaned back against the shaded side of the boulder. He was a single lonely figure, waiting. The gray, once-white robe, which if seen from any distance would seem just another rock, was his protection and shelter. He would wait now until the sun chariot had almost completed its journey before drinking again. He would travel all the coming night, and if nothing unforeseen occurred, he should make the distant mountains by the next sunrise.

He slept fitfully, a waking sleep that came and went. The silence was complete; only the omnipresent heat was his companion, though not a friend. He dozed, head jerking up now and then as he tried to seek the comfort of unconsciousness. He was still sweating and knew that that was a good sign; if the sweating were to stop, he knew a heat stroke would not be far away. As long as he could sweat, he was all right.

The seconds were minutes and the minutes were hours. Time seemed to stop, his mind in a torpor. He had no way of telling of the passing of the hours. It was too much of an effort to try and determine how long he had been sitting. He knew when the day began to cool, that would be the time to rise. Until then he would have to endure the dragging hours silently, helpless to speed them up.

Far across the desert and sea, another waited, silent and meditating in somewhat different surroundings. Marcus Aurelius, emperor of Rome, worried over how the Persian camping was progressing. Long ago, at the age of twelve, the emperor had embraced the teachings and severities of the Stoics. He had trained himself to place his body second to his mind, to resist passion in all forms, and to deal only in logic. For the Stoic, there were only two paths a man could take: the path to good or the path to evil. He regretted only that the office of state that he held so often forced him into unpleasant acts that he deemed necessary for the greater good. He personally had nothing against Christians, but they were a disturbing influence and preached a religion of weakness, which, if allowed to flourish, could sap the already vital strength of the empire.

Therefore, with a sigh of regret, he was now signing the order condemning another ten thousand of these followers of the crucified god to be put to death. He handed the instrument of death over to his chamberlain and took a drink of spring water. He avoided the use of wine or even eating to excess. In his mind, as the father of the Roman people, he had to set the example in everything. How else could he lead but by example, if he wanted the Roman people to return to the earlier state of nobility and virtue under which they had conquered most of the known world.

But, he sighed, he was sorely afraid that he was too late in coming on the scene. Still, one must try, and there was always the hope that his successor would be able to carry on with his work. Smiling, he thought of his son, Commodus—bright-eyed, brave, quick to learn, and the light of his father's eye. Yes, Commodus would carry on after him and lead the empire into an even greater age of prosperity and peace. Commodus would be the artist who would paint in the fine details of the future. He Marcus would now lay in the background with broad, sweeping strokes.

He rose and made his ablutions. It was time to preside over the college of priests and to perform sacrifices for the welfare of Rome and entreat the gods to grant them victory in all things. His wife, Lady Faustina, daughter of Antonius Pius, was waiting for him. She would not, of course, be permitted entry into the college. In her position, she would go to the Temple of the Vestal Virgins and make her own sacrifice and donatives.

Marcus Aurelius was blind to one thing, and that was the infidelity of his wife, who openly carried on with anyone she pleased and promoted her lovers to position of power. None dared tell the emperor otherwise, for to him, as he had written, she was the epitome of virtue. He would hear of nothing else. But his councillors knew, and indeed wondered if the boy Commodus had any of his father's blood in him. For the child, they knew, instead of being serious and gifted as was his father, was instead shallow of mind and purpose, taking on more the attitudes and directions of his mother than the rigid discipline of self-denial that the emperor espoused. The councillors dreaded the day Marcus would give the reins of the empire to his son.

The change in temperature brought Casca back from his dull, half-drugged sleep. He forced his eyes to open. The lids, dried and caked with grit and sweat, stung as he blinked to clear them. Rising from his shelter, he stood and faced the mountains, trying to lock the direction in his mind. If there was no moonlight tonight, and if there were no stars, there was certainly nothing else in the wasteland that he would be able to get a fix on to help guide him.

Long shadows were reaching across the plain of

stones from the gentle rises and hillocks. The sole
boulder became a sundial as its shadow reached
out twice its own length.

Casca shook his water skin. There was precious
little left. He took one full, long swallow and held
it in his mouth to let it soak into the gums and the
membranes of his throat, cutting some of the
buildup of phlegm and foul taste away. The bag
would be empty this night. He rewrapped his
burnoose about him and tied it at his waist.

The cooling of the evening was a balm to his
heat-reddened and flushed skin. It even helped to
ease the sore spots under his armpits and groins
where the grime and sand wore against his skin.
The dark closed around him like a soft, silent
blanket. He walked, the cool air giving him a sense
of renewed strength. The heat soon passed and
there were a few miles of stumbling over smooth,
slippery stones. Once, this must have been a lake or
an ocean bed. Several times he walked over shining
paths of salt that had collected into the low areas
where the waters must have evaporated or receded
back into the earth.

A few times he almost stepped on snakes, which
hissed and stuck out their tongues to taste the air,
then pulled back into sinuous twisting tendrils
ready to strike.

All that night, under clear but moonless skies, he
trekked toward the hoped-for shelter in the mountains. With stumbling steps, he met the new dawn
and looked to his objective.

It was still, to his eyes, as far away as it had been
on the previous day. As he had earlier noticed, distance was often deceptive in this land of shimmering waves of heat. His water was gone. He still car-

ried the empty bag with him in the hope that he might find a spring among the rocks or in the sand and would be able to refill it. He would not be able to rest much this day. If he stayed in one place too long, the heat would take what remained of his strength and he might not reach the walls of granite ahead. This day, heat or not, he must continue as long as he was able.

By midday, it felt as if Vulcan himself was pounding at his temples, trying to forge some strange weapon in his eternally burning furnace. The glare of the sun was a piercing, fiery dagger that lanced Casca's eyes. Every step was heavier than the last, but to stop was perhaps to never be able to go on. He stumbled blindly toward the mountains. A rock caught his dragging feet. It tore one sandal off and he fell to the earth, mouth open and panting, gulping in breaths of oven-baked air. He lay there for some time, trying to gather his inner resources together for the tremendous effort it would take to rise to his feet again. He lay still, mouth open and panting, eyes focused on a small gray stone, inches from his nose. A shadow moved over the stone. His eyes flicked up to meet another pair of goggle-wide eyes watching him. A large gray-and-brown-mottled lizard, the length of his foot, lay on its belly, mouth opening and closing like a fish. It was attracted by the flies beginning to gather around the form of the fallen man. Once and again, a long tongue flicked out and snared a victim faster than an eye could blink. It moved closer to his face and lay still, watching, one eye moving independently of the other. Casca's right hand, near his face, moved before he even thought of it and he held the lizard in his hand. He could feel the sinuous strength of its body squirming in his hand. Through silent lips he apologized for what he was about to do, then tore the beast's head off and placed the neck of the bleeding carcass between his cracked lips and sucked. He sucked the thin blood until the body of the lizard was drained, then tore it into pieces and chewed the meat slowly, squeezing every drop of moisture from the small cadaver. It wasn't much, but it was enough to give him the strength to rise once more to his feet.

He tossed what was left of the drained body of the lizard away and forced his mind on the hazy mountains.

He had to draw on every bit of his inner strength to take the first stumbling step. Fear aided him, too —the fear of what he would go through if he fell once more and was unable to rise. What would happen to him? He wouldn't be permitted to die; the Jew had seen to that. Would he just lie there and become a dried, desiccated husk that refused to die, condemned to a never-ending thirst and suffering?

That fear gave him a degree of increased fortitude and determination to go on. One dragging step after another, forcing his mind to concentrate on putting one foot in front of the other, he drifted into a semidrugged state that helped to ease the pain of his cut and blistered feet. He tried to lick his lips but found he couldn't force his tongue out of his mouth. It had swollen to twice its normal size and threatened to cut off his gasping and labored breathing.

His eyes were swollen almost completely shut and he thought for a time he was going blind when the day became darker and what little he could see

began to fade from sight. He stumbled into a
nearby bush and fell over onto his back. The bush
was in a dry riverbed. Feebly, he reached up to its
branches and felt them. They were hard to see. A
chill rushed over him from the evening breeze. At
least, he thought, I'm not blind. It's just the night
coming on. He touched the leaves, feeling their soft
green suppleness under his torn fingers.

Soft . . ? Up till now, everything in this pit of fire
that he had seen or touched had been dry and
rough! He tried to force his mind to work. It was
difficult! His mind kept wanting to slide off into
distant disjointed thoughts. With a tremendous effort he forced his concentration back to the bush.
It's green; the leaves are soft. It must be getting
moisture. Rolling over onto his belly, he began to
push the sand away from the roots of the bush.

Slowly, with an almost impossible effort, the
hole deepened. Casca put his face down into the
bottom of it and breathed deeply, ignoring the bits
of sand that were sucked up into his nostrils. He
could smell moisture. No! Smell wasn't quite right;
he could *taste* it with his mind. He tore a limb from
the bush to help him dig. Hours passed as he
worked in slow motion, but the hole deepened, and
soon he could feel the moisture with his fingers.
The rains that came so seldom to this region would
turn this dry bed into a raging torrent, and then
would disappear as fast as they had come. But
some of the water remained for this plant to feed
on and a few others.

The darkness was on him now, and still he
scooped out the sand until at last he could feel real
wetness. Sandy mud slid between his raw fingers.
He scooped up a handful of it and placed it in his

mouth, letting the wetness ease the pain and soak into his gums and tongue. He fought back an impulse to swallow the mud and sand. It helped, but it wasn't enough: he needed to drink. The hole wasn't filling with water; it was just wet sand muck.

Tearing off a patch of his tunic, he filled it with the sand and mud. Tying it into a bundle, he strained his neck, held the cloth to his mouth, and squeezed, forcing every ounce of strength remaining into his right hand and finally, through the cloth, came . . . *water!* A slow, sweet wetness that increased as he gained strength from the moisture. Again and again he refilled his rag and drank, nursing the wetness. As a child feeds at its mother's breasts, he sucked and was eventually filled.

He lay back then and slept, as his stomach dispersed the life-giving wetness throughout his body, feeding the cells and bringing back suppleness to dried tissue that had shrunk under the hammer of the sun. Two days he stayed by his miniature oasis, gathering his strength. At night, he found that if he stayed away from the hole for a while, other creatures would come to it, drawn by the smell of moisture in the night air. Rodents, lizards, snakes, and other vermin appeared. All were food and he wasted nothing. What he didn't eat was sliced into strips and put into the sun to dry. There wasn't much, but it was a great deal more than he had eaten for some time and would be enough, he hoped, to see him through.

He used much of his time squeezing his rag to fill his water skin, controlling the urge to drink it dry, and contenting himself with his damp rag. The water skin would be needed when he left, for he didn't know how long he would have to go before finding

more. The mountains rose over him. They were
stark, craggy, uneven piles of raw rock that
reached to the clear desert heavens. They seemed
like Hercules, carrying the weight of the world on
their granite shoulders.

Four days he stayed by his hole until he knew it
was time to leave. He was as strong as he would
ever be with the lack of real food. If he waited too
long the hole might run dry and the few animals
that came would disappear, and then he would be
back right where he started.

He waited for the dusk and once more began his
trek across the wastelands of the Persian desert.
But now, the mountains were his travel companions, and the wind that came from them in the
night talked to him of lost caravans and vanished
armies that had once followed this path. Some had
made it, but most lay forgotten under the shifting,
whispering dunes behind him. Their stories were
covered by the ever-changing sands that each year
claimed a little more of the arable lands, until one
day they would reach clear to the sea.

Several days passed as he made his way along the
boundary of the mountains heading west. He knew
he would have to come out of the desert at some
point; it could not be much further. He found small
springs in the shelters of the crags, which kept his
water skins filled. And . . . where he found water,
he found food.

At one such lonely watering hole he found two
horses grazing on the brush. A man, who Casca
presumed had been their owner, lay facedown near
the waterhole. Rolling the body over, the cause of
death was evident. The man's face was swollen to
half again its normal size, and there was a purple

color from the poison that had been injected into
his face through the two puncture marks on his
cheek. Probably a desert snake, lying near the hole,
had struck him while he'd been drinking. And,
Casca figured, it hadn't been too long ago. The
body showed no signs of decay yet and the horses
looked to be in fair shape.

He dug a shallow grave and covered the body
with stones. He said a general prayer for the man's
sake to whatever gods there were in this place, and
thanked him for the gift of the horses.

He rode out from the spot that night after check-
ing the packs. There was little in them but the
things a lonely traveler would need on the trail.
There were new clothes for him, though, and
packets of food to insure his reaching civilization
with at least a minimum of comfort. He followed
the trail back the way the man had come, moving
easily, letting the swaying of the horse rock him
into a light sleep as the miles were covered.

He felt a tingling up his spine on several occa-
sions after the first two days. It was a tingle that
says one is not alone, that eyes are watching.

But he never spotted anybody and put it down to
nerves. But the feeling still lingered, and from time
to time he thought that if he could just turn around
fast enough, he would be able to catch sight of the
watchers.

At night, he would search out crevices in the
rocks in which to build his lonely camp. A small
fire and saddle blankets provided him with all the
creature comforts he needed. The distant yapping
of a desert jackal would punctuate his thoughts,
and the isolation became almost a friend. He gathered it around him as he did his saddle blankets,

often spending long hours sitting on a rise looking out over the panorama of deserts and mountains. The wind was shifting and the cooler nights spoke of the end of summer. More frequently now, clouds would gather and let loose in the distance some of their jealously hoarded, life-giving rain. The few times it rained where he was, the Roman would raise his face to the drops, letting them clean the grit from his eyes and face, making no attempt to seek shelter.

There, standing on a ridge in the rain, overlooking the edge of the world, he felt as if he were the only man left in all creation. Would he in fact be that one day? Would he be all that was left of mankind? Or would the Jew claim him before that time came?

He shook the thoughts away; they were much too complicated for his mind. It would be better if he used his time to try and find out who had been following him. He was sure now. The feelings were just too strong. He knew they were out there somewhere.

That night Casca made camp in the open. He could not take shelter among the rocks because the trail he had been following had swung out some distance from them. The day had been long. He made a dry camp and contented himself with what was available. That night he sat close to the fire, made of dried horse droppings and dead twigs from the surrounding brush. His mind was drifting, but he tried to keep one ear cocked for any sound that wasn't natural. The fire and a half-full gut, though, soon lulled him into a nodding sleep. It was a sleep that ended in a flash of lights and pain as a thrown club smashed into the back of his head, sending him down into darkness.

As consciousness slowly returned, he wondered why the constellation of the Hunter whirled so rapidly in the heavens. It took a moment to shake his head free of the flashing, whirling lights and let it settle down into a deep throbbing, reminding him of several really bad hangovers he'd had over the years.

He got his first look at the new owners of his horses and property. They were two wild, scabby looking creatures with dark, weathered faces and coal-chip eyes that gave them the look of the Asian.

Small in size, their hair hanging in knotted masses to their waists, they grinned at him through black, gapped teeth that had been worn down almost to the gums from years of eating sand mixed in with their food. One was playing with Casca's sword while the other grinned a slant-eyed, death's-head leer at his trussed-up captive.

The smaller of the two gave him a kick and turned his attention to devouring everything remaining in the saddle bags that was edible. Their speech, if it could be called that, was mostly a series of grunts and gestures. They quickly got into an argument over the spoils, meager as they were, though to them it was a great treasure.

From the gestures they were making and the repeated looks in his direction, Casca figured that they were trying to decide what to do with him. One kept pointing to him and then to the small stack of silver and copper coins they had taken from his pack. The smaller of them obviously was trying to talk the other into selling him into slavery. His companion shook his head in the nega-

tive and made slashing movements with the short
sword. The one holding his sword went to Casca,
gave him a kick in the side, and pulled the Roman
up to his feet by the hair, poking and jabbing him
with the sword point. The other came over and the
two were quickly involved in a game of tug of war
over the sword.

Casca figured he'd better do something. The idea
of being sold back into slavery didn't particularly
appeal to him. He'd already, to his thinking, spent
entirely too many years in that miserable condition
and didn't look forward to a repeat performance.

Though his hands were bound behind him with
leather thongs, his feet were free, and he made
good use of them. While the two were determining
his fate, he gave one a snap kick to the balls that
raised the savage's testicles almost up to his belly
button. The other suffered a milder fate with a heel
to the jaw that splintered a few already rotted teeth
and probably saved him from a future toothache.

While the two thieves were wrapped up in their
own problems, Casca made use of the time to free
himself from his bonds, nicking himself only slightly in the process of handling a sword behind his
back.

When the two were able to motivate under their
own power, he sped them on their way with a few
well-placed slaps on the ass from the flat of his
blade. The two men wasted no time in putting as
much distance as possible between them and what
was to have been their victim. Casca gave his first
laugh in weeks at the sight of the bobbing heads
heading for the high ground.

The action of the attack and its subsequent outcome served to break him out of the dangerous,

mind-drugging lethargy that had been creeping over him. He was wide awake and ready for some living. Gathering his gear, he mounted his horse and with a kick to the flanks headed back into the wastelands, but this time his blood was racing and alive. There was a world to see, and, thanks to the Jew, he had what looked to be more than enough time to do it all. By the great brass balls of Jupiter, he would try.

Three more days and he reached the first signs of civilization. He came upon neat rows of cultivated fields and groves of olive trees. He spent a few scarce denarii for fresh meat and grain. After eating, he questioned the farmers and found that he had gone in a long half circle to the South and was now near the city of Aphrodisias.

He had heard of the city. It was well-known throughout the empire as an artists' colony, whose sculptures were to be seen in the finer domus of the empire. The city, as was obvious, was named for its patron goddess, Aphrodite, goddess of love and artists.

The farmers told him the city boasted of having the most liberal attitude toward sex of any in the empire, and also claimed to have more homosexuals to the square foot than any city in the world.

He spent four days in the city lying on his butt and taking it easy. He didn't have sufficient silver for the more plush boardinghouses, but after selling one of his horses he did have enough to raise a little hell and get laid a couple of times. He had some minor luck with dice, playing against Arab traders heading for Bithynia and won enough to cover the expense for part of the trip. He paid for the rest of it by renting out his sword as a guard for the caravan of Izmael Ben Torzah, a hawk-nosed old patriarch of the desert who looked like some great graying bird of prey, riding over the desert on his horse with his white robes flying loose about him in the wind.

The old man had taken a liking to the scar-faced Roman. When they were to leave the fleshpots of Aphrodisias, he went to the trouble of locating Casca and liberating him from the attentions of a widow, who was interested in having his knotted, muscled body carved into a likeness of marble. It would have been something new in the art field. It would have been called stark realism, since Casca was not one of the pretty boys of the Greek school but a real man with all his bad points—and, as she said when examining him in the nude, also his one good point.

Izmael paid the protesting woman no heed as he threw the half-naked and drunk carcass of his new guard over the back of one of his pack animals and rode off to join his caravan, already far outside the city and heading north.

When Casca finally sobered up, he wasn't sure whether to be grateful or not. He was sure he could have had a fairly decent existence as a male model. Hell, he had been getting into the thing. Learning to pose and twist his body into awkward positions while the matron supervised the sculpture. Too bad he had had to leave before it was finished. But what the hell, maybe another time.

After a little time passed, he realized that the life of a male model wasn't really what he was cut out for and forgave Izmael for hauling him off—especially when Izmael, himself feeling somewhat contrite, let Casca grade and sample the eight slave girls he was taking to the markets in Bithynia. On a scale of one to ten, two of them were threes, and the best one he gave an eight. The others fit somewhere in the middle. But all in all, they served their purposes well enough.

Casca didn't make it all the way with the caravan. When they stopped at Halicarnassus, on the coast, he got drunk with some sailors and woke up to find he had signed on as a crew man. The creaking of the timbers brought him staggering to the upper deck of the bireme, where he emptied the remains of the previous night's revelry into the Mediterranean. Being a fatalist, he reconciled himself to the change in his mode of travel. As long as they didn't try to chain him to an oar, he was as well pleased as could be expected.

The captain was fair and the food not too bad. They were carrying an amphora of grain and olive oil as well as hauling precut slabs of marble to be used as facings for public buildings in Rome. These they used as ballast to settle down the tendency of the galley to pitch and roll.

When they finally put into the port of Ostia, he chose to stay on board rather than take the time to visit the city of the Caesars. The last time he'd been here they had first put him in the arena, and then "Mad Nero" had sentenced him to life as an oar slave on the galleys of Rome. No, the Imperial City still had a bad taste for him and he stayed close to the ship, not venturing much further than the nearest tavern for a drink now and then. Finally they had reloaded their cargo holds and made sail. They sailed first to the west, then north, this time to Messilia in Gaul, where he had first enlisted as a boy in the legions.

He felt an increasing desire to be gone from the hot humid lands of the Mediterranean and also away from the Pax Romana. There was only one place he could go where the long arm of Roman law didn't reach—across the Rhine into Germania. He also wanted to see if what the mercenaries he had served from the northlands had said about the women was true. It was a poor reason, but who said you had to have a good one?

Casca felt a sense of relief when they finally left Ostia behind them and headed out again to the open sea and into the clean sea air. Here the stench of a decaying and corrupt empire would fade with the distance. Rome still left a bad taste in his mouth. At nights, when the sea was quiet and the bireme rocked to and fro with the swells, he would often awake with a jerk, his body soaked in cold sweat as memories rushed on him in his sleep. In his nostrils would be the sweet, sick smell of blood . . .

It was blood from the sands of the arena—the circus where he'd fought for the amusement of the Roman public, where women in a frenzy would sell themselves into slavery, making wagers on who would die. He could hear the voice of Corvu, the Lanista, barking out commands at the tyros, the same as a sergeant in the army would, constantly repeating commands to recruits until the response to orders became automatic.

"Don't go for the throat or the leg—hit the gut first. It's the biggest target. Cut the bastard after he's down. Remember, a leg wound might eventually slow a man up, but if you get careless he can still kill you. Play it safe. Only get fancy when you know he's through; then make it look tougher than

it is. Keep in mind that you're out there to enter-
tain the people, not get yourselves killed. Let the
bastards from the other schools do the dying."

But even Corvu was not above rigging a fight
against one of his own students if the man was a
troublemaker. It was simple enough to arrange. A
little draught of a sleeping drug in the cup of posca,
the watered vinegar that each gladiator would rinse
his mouth with before entering the arena, would
insure that in a few minutes the man's reaction
time would slow down. And before the audience
caught on that he was drugged, his opponent
would surely take advantage of the situation and
put a quick end to the unfortunate one.

But of all the faces of the arena, the one that
haunted him most was Jubala, the monstrous black
prince from Africa. He was a giant of a man, with
the strength and courage of a desert leopard, and
with a hatred in his heart that made him not just a
hunter, but a killer who fed his hate on pain and
death. . . .

So that even now, when the hortator of the
bireme struck the skin hide of the drum to set the
measure for the oarsmen, Casca could feel a twinge
seem to ripple over his back, for a slave master's
lash, on the galley he had slaved on, had made its
mark there. All this, he owed to Rome. But still, he
was a Roman.

When they reached Messilia, Casca transferred
over to a grain ship heading up the Rhone to
Lugdunum, again trading the muscles in his back
and arms for passage. Leaving the barge at
Lugdunum, he took a large portion of his remaining sesterces and bought a young gray ass to carry
what wealth he had on its small back, and struck

out, trying to avoid contact with any of the Roman garrison along the way. After all, he was still a deserter and the arm of Rome is as long as her roads, reaching from Asia to Britannia. He didn't really understand why he wanted to cross the Rhine into Germania, but his feet took him to the same spot where he had killed his first man. Was that it?

Had he come back here because this was where he'd become a soldier, where his sword for the first time had cut the life out of another human? The number he had taken since that day, he couldn't recall. Only rarely did a face stand out in his mind for a moment, then fade back into the mists of the past where they belonged. . . . Perhaps forgetting helped him to keep his sanity. If all the slaughter and pain he had inflicted and suffered himself were to come to him at one time, it would be too much for his mind to stand. Perhaps forgetting was the way the mind cured itself of the sickness that could linger with bad memories.

It was with a sense of something yet to come that he reached the banks of the Rhine just before nightfall. It was too late to make a crossing now; he would have to wait until the morning. He cast a regretful look at his ass and sighed. There was no way he would be able to get the animal across the rushing waters. . . . So, waste not, want not. And it *was* time for chow.

Chapter One

Casca watched the broad back of Glam Tyrsbjorn as the ox of a man moved with amazing silence through the brush and tall forest. His double-handed sword hung from a sling on his back and a single-bladed axe dangled from a thong on his side. In his hand, he carried a spear made for the killing of wild pigs, but it served as well for men.

Glam was the first man he'd met when he came out of the waters of the Rhine and then, the red-nosed, oversized hunk of sausage had wanted to rob him and leave him all but naked. What was it I called him that pissed him off so much . . . ? *Turnip dick,* that's it!

He had conned Glam into putting down his weapons and letting the Roman come out of the water to fight him with bare hands. Glam was big, even for a barbarian, but the Roman had learned something about fighting with empty hands that the barbarians of the dark woods had no concept of. They only knew to hit and smash or, if you were strong enough, to grab your opponent and squeeze his ribs until they caved in. Glam's brute strength was no match for the few techniques taught Casca by the yellow philosopher from beyond the far In-

dus river, where the priests learned to defend themselves without the aid of anything more than their
own hands and feet. True, Shiu Lao Tze had not
taught Casca a great deal, but what he had was
more than enough to make him a match for anyone
he had met so far on this side of the world.

But Casca also knew that if he screwed up and
missed one of his movements, a good blow could
knock him down. And no matter who it was, if you
were landed a really good shot, the odds were you
would get your brains kicked out, tricks or no
tricks. Since then, he and Glam had become sword
companions and Glam had been his guide and
teacher. The gruff bear of a man was basically
good-natured and, once he had gotten over being
peeved at Casca for whipping his butt, he became a
fast and good friend. They'd had no more disputes
since that day when, after tossing Glam into the
Rhine, he had threatened to braid the big
German's legs if he didn't behave himself. When
Glam had considered the effect that this act would
have had on his sex life, he'd rapidly agreed to a
truce.

But now there was something else happening
ahead of them that demanded their attention. The
sun was up only an hour and low mist swirled
around the roots of the giant pine and fir trees
twisting up into the morning sky. They were like
ghostly tendrils, which some of the legends spoke
of as being the spirits of fallen warriors eternally
searching to find their way to the great Halls of
Valhalla.

A touch of smoke mixed with the vapors. Barely
audible were the distant sounds of dying. Shrill
screams from women and children mingled with

the deeper grunts of men killing each other. Casca raised his face to smell the mist, to search out the direction of the cries. In these dark primordial forests, sounds were hard to pinpoint.

He loosened his sword in its scabbard and took his small, round, hide-covered buckler with a brass boss in the center from the pack on his back.

The gray-blue eyes sparked with anticipation. His companion, that monstrous bear of a man who, from a distance could have been easily mistaken for one wrapped as he was in the hides of those beasts, swung his single-bladed axe from his shoulder and ran a calloused finger over the edge. Glam, son of Halfdan the Ganger, wiped his other hand on his bristled beard to get rid of any sweat so he could get a better grip on his broad-bladed boar spear. "Do we go?"

Casca nodded his head in the affirmative. They knew that the sounds of battle in the distance were probably instigated by the members of the Quadii, who had been raiding far from their tribal lands.

More than once since the snows had gone they had come across the mountain passes to leave gutted and burned villages behind them, taking with them only the women and children. The rest were put to the sword. The women and children brought high prices in the slave markets. The survivors would find themselves being offered for sale, time and again, many going as far as the slave pens of Rome or even Alexandria in Egypt. Fair hair and blue eyes brought high prices and Germans were known to make good slaves if you could catch them young enough.

Wary and tense, they moved through the woods. Everything around them was covered in a rich, lush, green haze from the wild undergrowth of ferns and brush. Ground fog danced between their legs as they moved to the sounds of the slaughter.

Casca advanced with no sense or feeling of injustice for the people being taken as slaves. After all, slavery was the natural order of things. He had even been one a couple of times himself. No, it was the killing of the women and children and helpless old people that pissed him off. There had always been slavery and probably always would be. It was a person's fate to be one or not.

Besides, he didn't like the raiding tribesmen very much anyway, and it gave him an excuse to work out some of his frustrations on them. Glam had said it was not good to keep one's feelings bottled up inside. It could drive a man crazy if he wasn't able to express himself fully. Therefore, it was much better to do just what you felt like and let your feelings come to the surface with a little healthy killing. Besides, there was always the chance of picking up a little booty along the way. . . .

Several shadows moved out of their way, back into the brush. The sounds of fighting brought others to the scene. The forest wolves had long since learned that smoke and screams meant that soon food would be had. They gathered now to wait until the sounds quieted down. Then they would have their turn to feed on the remains of those left behind. These wolves had grown brave of late. They had learned to dispel some of their fear of man by finishing off the wounded and those too weak to fight back. At first the wolves would take a tentative bite, then jump back to see if their meal had any fight left in them. If there was no retaliation, they would go in for the kill. After a few times they learned not to wait. Human blood was not their favorite, but it was easy to get, and the meat, though saltier than that of the forest deer, would still fill empty bellies and give the pups something to cut their teeth on. And now anyone who left the confines of his or her village alone was considered fair game.

The leader of the pack sniffed at the scent of the two intruders, his gray muzzle wrinkling back to show long yellow canines. He gave a low whine and his pack moved away from the two men with steel in their hands. He knew it would be best to leave these humans alone. Killers always recognized each other. They would be content to wait for easier prey. It wouldn't be long. They licked their muzzles and cleaned their paws. Soon they would feed, but for now they would wait. . . .

The smell of smoke thickened. If there had been no mist it would have been easily visible rising up to the tops of the trees to blow away into the morning sky. The sounds of fighting had died down to an occasional scream as the raiders took their pleasure with the women of the doomed village.

Casca and Glam crawled into some brush, the sweet clean smell of damp greenery contrasting with the odors of violent death coming to them from across the small clearing. Lying on their bellies, they could see about twenty dwellings in various stages of being burned, but most were already no more than piles of smoldering embers. The low stockade surrounding the houses had been designed to serve more as a fence to keep their livestock in than slavers out.

The slavers were moving their cargoes out. They were hooked together with ropes of braided hide connecting them together at the neck. They had been broken down into age and sex categories: children on one line at the rear, women in the center, and a few surviving adult males in the front. All of them totaling about thirty, stumbled out of what had been only minutes before, their homes. . . .

Of the males, only two appeared to be out of their teens. The other four varied in age, anywhere from twelve to fourteen. Their new owners were rough-looking men, wearing mixtures of hides and armor. Several wore homemade imitations of Roman helmets that they had decorated with the horns of animals or wings of birds. All wore long untrimmed beards of various colors. The throwing axe was carried along with a Gallic-styled sword, one longer than that of the legions', but shorter than the one preferred by the Suevii tribesmen or the Marcomanni.

Once they were clear of the village, Casca and Glam moved in to see if there was anything worth saving. Only a few broken pots were left among the ruins. Bodies in broken positions lay scattered about the smoldering ruins. That the invaders had not had things go completely their way was evident by the number of them lying about with ripped out stomachs and throats. They too had been stripped of anything of value and left for the wolves to clean up. Several were lying on top of women. They had died in the process of rape. A short-bladed knife broken at the hilt in the hand of a young blonde-haired girl showed how it was done. The rest of the blade was between the ribs of her ravager.

Everything in the village had been slaughtered, from the cattle down to the dogs and children. Glam helped Casca gather the bodies together in a pile, then collected what unburned wood they could find and stacked it around the bodies. Sweat-

ing after their labor, they took a smoldering brand
and blew it back into life. The funeral pyre burned
bright and the fresh smell of new fire made the
wolves in the forest whimper. They knew they
would have to wait a little longer, and the smell of
burning flesh told them there wouldn't be as much
to feed on as they had hoped for.

A slow drizzle started to wet down the furs on
both of their bodies, cleaning off the traces of soot
from their faces. They followed after the raiders,
knowing it would be best to wait until the hours
just before dawn so they could see what they could
do against the forty-odd barbarians. Time would
be their ally. It was about all they had—that and a
desire to let their weapons taste the blood of those
they followed. . . .

The slavers made camp shortly before nightfall
in a grove of oaks by the edge of a clearing. They
tied their slaves to trees, having three men guard
them full-time. The leader of the slavers selected a
young female for his pleasure and let the others
share the remaining women—after the slaves had,
of course, tended to the women's work of making
campfires and preparing meat.

From a safe distance, Casca and Glam lay on
their bellies watching the movements around the
fire. The smell of meat cooking set their mouths
watering. They had not had food for two days—
not since they had eaten their last horse, or, at
lease, since Glam had eaten it. Casca had consumed only a few pounds of the lean red meat
while Glam gulped one chunk after another until
Casca thought his savage friend's gut would stretch
permanently out of shape. There were only a few
scraps left now.

Right now Glam was grumbling under his

breath about how he could devour one of the forest
bears, hides, claws, and all, and Casca believed
him. When it was empty, Glam's stomach had a
habit of making sounds not dissimilar to the noises
made by feeding hogs. There were too many of
them for a direct attack, so they decided to take
their time and wait for anyone that got careless or
straggled. If they got one or two a night, it
wouldn't take too long before they had the odds
down to levels they could manage.

Fortunately enough, the rain had eased off to no
more than thin, vaporous drizzles that only served
to keep them damp and cold.

Glam nudged Casca's ribs gently enough to cave
in the ribs of an ox and pointed one long, black-
nailed finger off to the side of the grove. A single
barbarian was hauling a woman off to the bushes.
Glam grunted . . . probably a shy type, or he's built
so bad he doesn't want anyone else to see his defi-
ciencies. They gave their quarry time to get settled
into his work over the female, and then slipped on
each side of him just as he finished and was raising
himself off the unresisting female. She had given
him scant pleasure, just lying there with no movement or emotion; but for his needs that served just
as well.

The barbarian was involved with tying up his
leather breeches when Glam's hands went around
his throat. Cutting off any sound, he raised the
man clear from the ground and twisted. The crack
of the neck breaking was muted. The girl lay still,
eyes closed. She wasn't even aware that her abuser
was already on his way to whatever hell his race
believed in.

Chapter Two

Casca covered the girl's mouth with his hand. She didn't move, thinking it was another of the slavers come to take their turn at her.

"Be still, make no sound. We'll have you away from here soon enough." The voice was different from the guttural grunts of the speech of the Quadii. She opened her eyes to see a stern, scarred face looking down at her. Her eyes glimpsed to the side where she saw the body of her tormentor lying with a crooked neck and a hairy giant of man going through his victim's pouch. Casca helped the girl to her feet. She didn't have to get dressed. The savage had wasted no time on niceties; he'd just pulled her homespun dress up and gone to it. A couple of words to Glam and the giant heaved the rapist's carcass over his shoulder as if it were a gutted hog and moved back into the cover of the woods.

Casca and the girl followed. As swiftly as the terrain permitted, they put distance between themselves and the slavers' encampment. One was enough for now; they would hunt again later. By taking the body with them, there was the chance that the raiders would think their comrade had merely run off with the girl to sell her separately and keep the gold for himself.

They hadn't covered much ground before they heard voices calling for their missing comrade. Glam dropped his load under a group of bushes and covered the body with leaves and branches.

That night they ate a cold handful of uncooked grain and the last scrap of the horsemeat. Before night fell, the girl took time to search among the trees for herbs and plants. Finding what she needed, she waited until they stopped for the night, and then began to eat her collection of green things. Casca said nothing, content to leave her to her own devices. After about an hour, she began to cramp, drawing her legs up to her chest then jerking them back again. When Casca asked if he could help, she said between gritted teeth that what she had taken was insurance that she would not give birth to a slaver's bastard and that the cramp would end soon enough.

They huddled in their furs half sleeping, one ear cocked for any unusual sound. Glam had given the girl the filthy hide coverings of the corpse to use. Stinking as they were, they did serve to keep out the worst of the night chill. Several hours before dawn, Casca made the others rise and get ready to move out. He had thought about the situation and decided to get ahead of the slavers and see if there was anyplace on the trail that would serve as an ambush site. The girl stayed behind the Roman's back, keeping close to him, with her face down to avoid whipping branches. Glam broke trail, somehow always seeming to know which way to go, even in the almost complete darkness of the woods.

At dawn they stopped by a narrow creek to drink and rest. The girl took advantage of this to wash as much of the filth off her as she could.

Glam cast an admiring glance at the girl as she bathed nude in the stream. Nudity was nothing to be ashamed of in her tribe. And after a little scrubbing, she looked a lot better. Before, her hair had a dull, drab look to it, but after rinsing out the ashes and dirt, it took on a healthy auburn color. She was small but well-built and toned. The girl told them that there was only one way through the passes, which the tribesmen had to take, and, like Glam, she had an instinct for direction that civilized man could never hope to attain. One had to be raised in these forests to acquire that kind of sense. Glam grunted and threw his pack up a little higher and they moved again. This time Casca was leading, following Glam's instructions. All that day they kept moving, until finally they approached the entrance to the mountain's passes, which led back to their lands. Casca figured they were three or four hours ahead of the slavers, who would be held back by their human cargo. The trio had time. And most likely the raiding party would make camp outside the walled entrance to the mountains. The steep cliffs and narrow defiles gave an enemy too many opportunities for ambush to be risked.

Following Casca's orders, Glam and the girl spent the rest of the time before nightfall searching for saplings of ash or oak. Casca would have a use for them that night. . . .

Glam and the girl moved further up into the passes, where they built a small fire. There they cut and sharpened the ash and oak poles into spiked stakes and hardened the points over the fire. Casca kept watch.

Waiting, he let his mind drift while watching the racing clouds gather overhead among the high peaks. Occasionally shafts of gold light broke through and lanced the earth below. He sat on a gentle incline near the entrance. Below him was a clearing through which his prey had to come. A distant sparkle caught his eye: a gleam of light had bounced off polished metal. They were coming.

Casca left his perch and ran up the pass to warn Glam and the girl. Tying their bundles of sharpened stakes together with a strip of leather, they moved back down to where they could keep an eye on the approaching party.

The leader of the group, after crossing the clearing, held up his hand to signal a halt. He wore a bell-shaped iron helmet with the horns of a goat protruding out of it at angles. A big man and tough, he hadn't survived this long by not having an instinct for danger. Something about the pass bothered him. Besides, it would be warmer here on the lowlands in shelter of some rocks. They could build their campfires and feed with a degree more comfort here than in those high passes where the wind ripped and tore at every piece of exposed skin. Casca nodded, pleased with himself for correctly deducing the barbarian leader's course of action. They would camp outside the pass.

Glam and the girl followed him to the sheltered cleft in the rock wall. There they huddled together to wait and rest and wait for the dark.

The enveloping darkness would be their ally this night—that and the sharpened stakes. They slept, the girl dreaming of dark thoughts of revenge while Glam muttered in his sleep for more beer and meat, making smacking, sucking noises. Casca stayed awake, eyes half open, letting his body relax. Taking in one deep breath and then letting it out slowly, he eased the tension.

He and Glam had come a long way since they had first met on the banks of the Rhine, a long way from that river to where they were now, near the borders of Pannonia. How far they would go together was yet to be seen. But so far Glam had been as good as his word. He had told the smaller Roman that he would show him all this land had to offer—even to the steppes of Scythia. There the Alani tribes were slowly being pushed back by gnomish invaders from the east, who never removed themselves from their horses' backs unless it was to take a crap.

These tribes were called by the rest of the western world the Huns. Glam had met them before when working as bodyguard to one of the Alani kings. He swore they even made love on horseback. When they walked they looked like trolls, with their legs twisted and undersized from so many years in the saddle. On horseback, they were . . . unbeatable. On the ground they were helpless in the way a crippled wolf was. You could kill them easily as long as you kept out of the way of the snapping jaws.

These Huns were the vanguard of a great migration that had begun a hundred years before when a great king of Han defeated them and drove them from their trivial lands to wander. And in the wandering, they had gained new strength as they followed the grass. When they met a new tribe, they either destroyed it or took it in with them to swell what was called the Horde. . . .

It was not uncommon anymore to find men from

a dozen races riding under the horse and yak-tailed
standards of the Khans. They would even take the
name of Hun for themselves and emulate their
dwarfed masters in every act of cruelty known.
Glam swore that one day they would come out of
the east by the tens of thousands, and when that
day came, there would be enough bloodshed to
drown even the Seven Hills of Rome.

When there were still about three hours to dawn,
Casca rose and stretched out his legs and arms,
breathing in deeply the crisp air of the highlands.
He shook his head to clear it of the half-dreams
and mist. Speaking softly, he woke Glam and the
girl. It occurred to him that he had never asked her
name. Glam and the girl each woke in their own
manner. Glam, grumbling about food, walked to
the edge of the cleft and urinated. The girl gathered
their bundles of stakes together and stood ready to
leave. Her movements were quick and eager. The
woman wanted blood and, as Casca well knew, a
female was far more dangerous when she had the
upper hand than any man was. He touched the thin
scar running from his left eye to the corner of his
mouth. Indeed, it was best to always keep one eye
on a woman—especially if you thought you had
done something to piss her off. . . .

Chapter Three

The three moved together back down the darkened gorge like a cat on a hunt, quick and intent. Glam, for all his size, was as surefooted as a mountain goat. And the girl had been born to these parts. Casca was the one who stumbled a couple of times; he swore under his breath each time, until the girl told him to shush. Chastened, he obeyed. Whoever got this one for a wife was in for a rough time. He grinned at the thought that maybe the worst punishment possible for the man who raped her might have been to make him marry her in accordance with the laws of the tribes. That would really have taught him a lesson. Nothing quick like having your neck snapped, but the long, lingering agony of a nagging wife's tongue.

The Quadii had made camp in a rough circle in a sheltered area surrounded by large boulders about sixty feet across. The male slaves were kept together under the watchful eye of three guards. The rest of the perimeter was walked by another four. Casca removed his sword belt and scabbard and carefully laid them on the ground. He didn't want to take any chance on anything making noise. He kept his sword in his right hand, ready for use.

Glam held his axe close to his side. The moonless night gave them good cover as they crept and crab-crawled closer to the camp. The only light came from a smoldering fire in the center. Casca tried to make sure the leader was bedded down, but no luck. In the dark there was no way to make out one hairy mass from another.

The girl stayed close behind them carrying the bag of stakes. Making their way around the edge of the surrounding boulders, they came down on the side where the male captives were kept. The women had been separated from them and were being kept on the other side of the fire with the children. Inch by inch they moved in, slowly, carefully, reaching the side of the boulders nearest the prisoners. Casca removed his helmet and set it aside. He whispered to Glam and the girl. They nodded agreement and he lay back on his belly. The feel of the damp grass was cool, soaking through his robes. He crawled, keeping his body as close to the rocks as possible, one yard, then another.

The prisoners were darkened masses lying together in huddled clumps. Casca watched the guards. When they turned to walk away, he rolled silently into the body of the male captives, becoming one with the dark. He moved close to a young man, who grumbled in his fitful sleep at the movement. His eyes jerked open with a terrified snap when a strong hand clamped over his mouth and held him still. A strange voice whispering in his ear quieted him. He nodded his head under the restraining hand and he was released. A gentle tugging at his bonds and his wrists were cut free. He didn't move. He just lay in the same position and bumped his head against his neighbor until the

man woke, protesting. A few soft, quick words and
he too was silent while another body moved close
to him to free his hands and press a short knife into
them. Moving as if still asleep, he twisted and cut
his feet free. The two prisoners, obeying the
stranger's orders, each woke the man next to him,
spoke, then freed him, passing him a knife to do
the same to his neighbor, until all six were free.
They waited, keeping their same positions, lying as
still as possible. Being this close to freedom, it was
hard not to break and run.

Casca took his bundle of stakes out of his robes
and handed them over to be passed around to the
men. While he was doing this, the same action had
been repeated on the women's side of the camp by
the girl. The prisoners were free. Now they had to
take out the sentries. Casca whispered in the ear of
the young man he had just freed. He knew the
youngster was grinning, even though it was too
dark to see his face.

Casca snapped his fingers twice. The sound
brought Glam to a standing position behind the
boulder; it also brought two of the guards closer.
They weren't suspicious, only curious. These two
would be Casca's and the youngster's meat tonight.
Glam was already moving around the other side of
the boulder to take out the remaining sentry. A distant, wet thump told Casca that Glam had reached
his target and the axe had fallen.

Glam held the man's body up so it wouldn't
make any sound falling. He dragged it back into
the shadows and quickly stepped out to take his
place, careful to stay in the shadows away from the
fire so that his face and size wouldn't give him
away. The dull sound of their comrade dying

turned the other two around in their tracks. Hesitant and uneasy, they fingered their weapons. One called out softly, "Madorg, you all right?" The figure in the shadows raised an arm with Madorg's spear in it and waved back. They both sighed, tension released, and began to walk their rounds again.

Casca nudged the young man next to him and slowly turned onto his belly. Gathering his legs under him, he held the short sword to the ground where it couldn't be seen and slowly raised himself from the earth as the two guards turned their backs to the captives and began to walk back toward the other side. The youngster did likewise. The others kept their positions. Taking a deep breath, Casca moved on the nearest man. One knotted, muscled arm went around the raider's throat, cutting off any cry as the broad blade of the short sword penetrated his back on the right side of the spine. Angled up, it crossed over and severed organs until it reached the heart, nearly cutting it in half.

The youngster had moved, too. He had his man on the ground, the short blade of the knife buried in his back and a hand over his mouth. He was trying to keep him still. The son of a bitch would not die. The youngster struck again and again, driving the knife in, but his man kept fighting, trying to get the hand away from his mouth. He succeeded in sinking his teeth into the youngster's hand and bit down, trying to chew clear through to the bone. His efforts were terminated when Glam's axe took the back of his skull off.

The rustling of the dying guard woke one of his comrades, who was a light sleeper. The man called out, asking if everything was all right. Glam spoke in a stage whisper, "Shut up and go back to sleep." The warrior rolled, mumbling about Madorg being a grouchy son of a bitch, and went back to sleep.

On the women's side, the girl was waiting. . . . Casca made his way back around the perimeter until he was just behind the boulders where the women were kept. He snapped his fingers twice and the girl was ready to do her part. She and three others would take out their guards in a way that women knew best. She gave the signal and she and the three women she had chosen quickly removed their clothing, and, nude, lay down on the ground on their backs.

When the guards turned, they saw the young women lying there, their breasts and thighs glowing in the light of the campfire. The warriors gaped, openmouthed. This was something new! Rape they were familiar with, but not this! How the women had freed themselves of their bonds never entered their minds. All they could see were the young women running their hands over their naked bodies, moaning softly, opening their legs and squirming at their feet.

Stupefied, the guards each went to the girl nearest him; eyes wide in dirty bearded faces, they lay their weapons aside to remove their pants. The girls whispered to them to be silent so as not to wake the others. Grunting, the guards removed their pants and fell into the waiting arms of the girls. They were moaning and giggling softly, which the guards mistook for pleasure.

The warriors began to work, their minds on nothing but the sweet woman flesh writhing in mock pleasure beneath them. They were still involved when they died. When the girls, still lying on their backs, looked up and saw Casca and Glam standing over them, accompanied by two men from their village, they smiled and struck out with the sharpened stakes that they had been lying on. As they struck, so did the men. Axes and knives quickly finished off the four guards. The women enjoyed the death tremors of their savage lovers and held them near until it ceased. Then they rolled out from beneath the dead men and spat in their faces. Casca was right. There was nothing like the hatred of a woman.

The other women, all freed now, rose from the ground to join their sisters. The steel weapons of the guards were distributed among the men, and sharpened stakes given to each of the other women after they'd undressed.

In spite of the night chill, all felt a warmth in their bellies. The men moved back into the shadows spreading out around the camp. Casca asked one of them where the headman of the raiders slept. A pointing finger showed where the man with the horned helmet lay under a skin shelter, alone.

Casca moved near, standing directly behind the headman's sleeping place. The women waited until they saw his sword flash gold in the light of the campfire as he waved a signal. Then they moved. Each one crept silently until she had reached her objective; then each lay down beside the sleeping man. Quietly, easily, their mouths silenced any protest from those who woke at the feel of a naked body lying next to them. When they were all in place, Casca filled his lungs and yelled, his voice echoing across the valley, *"Kill!"*

And, *kill* they did! Wooden stakes struck deep

into stomachs and hearts. The freed men finished off the few that managed to escape the wrath of the women. Grim butchers! Work was done this night.

The headman rolled out of his shelter, instantly alert, weapon ready. He gaped for a moment at the sight of the women killing his men, then roared in anger and lurched forth, long sword swinging. His sword hand was stopped in midair as Casca moved quickly behind him and grabbed his wrist. Swinging the barbarian around, Casca grinned a look of killing and spat, "Sing your death song, hero." He drove his short sword into the man's gut, angling the blade up. He struck so hard that he raised the man clear off his feet. Grabbing the man by the hair, he forced him to his knees and moved his sword hand down. Drawing the blade out in a long, smooth slice, he opened the chieftain's stomach from chest to groin letting the hot, steaming intestines fall in a convoluted mass, wet and quivering, to the ground.

The chieftain never had a chance to sing his death song. His mouth had filled with his own blood before he could open it.

Several of the raiders had not yet died and their former slaves were in no hurry to put them in that blessed state. The women gathered around them, dragging them nearer to the campfire.

Casca knew what was going to happen next. Even he, with all the fighting he had been in and the slaughter he had seen, had no stomach for what lay in store for the raiders. But this was their way, and the only way he could have stopped it was to kill the women. Besides, they had earned the right to return the pain and humiliation they had suffered to those they now held down beside the fire.

Casca moved away into the shadows to wait until it was over. He knew that it would be several hours before the last wet, gurgling screams stopped.

The women went to work. With sharpened stakes and blades heated to red-hot over the fire's coals, they cut and they sliced, taking their time, making sure their victims would feel every second of agony before they died.

It was dawn before the last raider was permitted to die. He didn't scream. His mouth had been filled, first with red-hot coals and then with his own testicles shoved down his throat until he strangled.

The women were through. They sat, tired, haggard, their bloody hair in knots, their faces drained.

It was over!

Casca and Glam left the women and their men to return to what was left of their village. Several of the women had offered themselves to the two, but after seeing how their last lovemaking had ended, not even Glam had any desire for a quickie with the still bloody-handed maidens.

They were content to take what they wanted from the bodies and baggage of the Quadii and leave the rest for the villagers. What they took were the easy-to-carry items, and that wasn't much, plus a few pieces of well-worn small coins of gold and silver to help see them through the season.

Both of them were glad to leave behind this last bit of gruesome business. They had no sympathy for the women's victims, but even so, it was still a little hard to warm up to a girl who had just cut off and shoved a man's family jewels down his throat.

A quick farewell and they headed over the pass, taking the same route the raiders would have. Any direction was better than none.

For the rest of the warm months they wandered from one tribal ground to the next, and Casca marveled at the vast expanses they'd covered where no man had ever seen a Roman. The tribes numbered men in masses too great to count. He believed the women of Germania didn't give birth to one child at a time; they had litters instead.

From others, they heard of the migration of a tribe of fierce warriors from Scandia. For years now they had been moving to the warmer regions south of them—a trickle at first, then a flood that would soon reach the boundaries of Rome. Casca wondered what would be the result when Rome met the tribes of the Goths in their full strength and numbers.

They went as far east às the northern border of Pannonia, crossed the river Danube, and spent a couple of pleasant weeks in the fleshpots of Vienne, enjoying the comforts of a city somewhat civilized by the Romans, who garrisoned the frontier along the Danube. From there, before the winter caught them, they moved back to the east along the banks of the river. For a time they detoured from the river to travel through the high mountains with their lofty summits of eternal snow, down through deep, green valleys where a man's whisper could be heard echoing a dozen times until it finally faded in the clear mountain air.

But they didn't want to stay in these high, beautiful mountains for long. If winter found them there, they wouldn't be able to get out until the next year's thaw opened up the passes. They moved on. The journey from the place of the slaughter of the Quadii raiders was one huge horseshoe that brought them back near the Rhine and the edges of the Hyrcanian forests. They were near the city of Colonia Agrippina on the Rhine, across the river from the lands of Tencteri, when the first snows came. Large flat flakes fell gently from the sky— one, then another, gradually increasing until the men were blinded by the brilliance of a blanket of pure white snow.

They kept to the German side of the Rhine until they reached the bank opposite Vetera, the last major Roman town before the Rhine emptied into the sea. Even now, large chunks of ice could be seen drifting with the current toward the greater waters separating Britannia from the continent.

After a certain degree of haggling they found a fisherman that agreed to ferry them across the river. There was nothing on the German side to make them want to stay. There were a few homesteads and trading posts, but there were still too many members of hostile tribes around. Casca had decided that if they were going to get any rest or supplies they had better try to do it on the Roman side of the river.

By the time they reached midstream, a full winter storm was on them. Raging, gusting winds tried to turn the shallow boat over and dump its passengers into the frozen flow. But the captain of the small boat knew his craft, and without much anxiety, though his passengers were definitely uneasy, he beached his craft on the Roman side, took his pay in the form of two small pieces of silver and one of copper, and hurriedly left, heading back for the German side of the Rhine.

Casca and Glam hauled their belongings onto their shoulders and walked through deserted dirt streets, now frozen hard from winter. The blasting winter wind and whipping snow pushed them along. Anyone with any sense at all was inside out of the cold. But they had no choice. They wandered for a while through the streets, leaving their footprints behind them in the new ice crust until Glam raised his nose like a hunting hound and said in a reverent voice, as he sniffed the air, "Beer. I smell beer and roasting meat."

Casca raised his nose to do as Glam had and all he got was a nose full of falling snow, which made him sneeze.

Glam clucked at Casca's obvious disability and deficiency in the olfactory senses and led the way unerringly to a wooden door. "This is it," he informed his companion.

Chapter Four

Glam entered the smoky confines of the tavern
first, and Casca followed. Once inside, they shut
the wooden door behind them and, like dogs,
shook their bodies to rid their shoulders and furs of
the snow that had gathered on them. The smoke
from the fireplace and oil lamps bit at their eyes
and nostrils. It took them a moment to adjust to
the new dimmer lighting after the stark brilliance
of the whiteness outside.

Since they'd entered, other eyes had been watching them. They were sizing up the new guests, while
doing a mental tally of how much they would be
worth and if the value would be worth the effort.
And the watchers were deciding against any trouble with these two. The giant German's size alone
was enough to discourage all but the most
foolhardy, and his friend had a hard look in his
eyes that said he was well-familiar with death and
had drunk of the cup of pain more than once and
survived.

The two made their way through the mixed company of border thieves and outcasts. It was easy to
read their faces, for they had one thing in common:
the feral look of givers of pain for pain's sake.

They found a spot near the fire and threw their robes off to lie steaming in front of the open hearth. Keeping their weapons close at hand, they moved a bench around and situated themselves with their backs to the wall so that they could keep a ready eye on the rest of the guests in this haven of murderers and thieves.

The food was plain but filling. The wine was as sour as the beer, but they both agreed it beat the hell out of trudging back through the bitter wind and snow in search of food and drink.

Talking quietly, they too sized up the opposition in the room, mentally cataloging those that would most likely give them trouble. A burst of frigid air from the sudden opening of the door attempted to blow out the fire in the hearth. A new figure stood in the darkened doorway, his body outlined from what little light there was outside, for the snow's brilliant reflections were fading as night began to fall.

A low murmur ran through the crowd of other watchers. The newcomer was of different stock than the two warriors near the fire. He wore expensive robes of fine cloth and had jeweled rings on his fingers, both silver and gold.

Then a smaller figure stepped out from behind the man—a boy of perhaps ten years, with fine features and curled hair cut short. He took the man's hand to lead him inside and looked over the crowd of hoodlums with wide, intelligent eyes that showed no trace of fear.

The man was near sixty, with hair as white as the snow outside and a body, though now stooped with years, that had once been much larger and stronger. The broad remnants of massive shoulders, the long arms, and the knotted, scarred hands said that once this had been a man to be reckoned with. But now, to the scum that were watching, he was something to amuse themselves with for a while and then to divide among the strongest. In this place he could only be considered as dead meat.

An impulse made Casca move from his seat. Hand on his sword, he quickly approached the newcomers in the doorway, jovially calling out with seeming familiarity, "Well, it's about time you showed up. We thought you and the boy had lost yourselves in the storm. Come on over . . . we have a table ready and we'll get some food into your cold bellies soon enough." He hustled the two in front of him, giving them no chance to speak or protest, and ushered them to the bench.

Smiling, Glam rose to make room for them. He'd understood Casca's intentions from the first. The boy chose to sit beside Glam, his tiny body dwarfed by the giant's, making them each look more and less than they were.

Keeping alert for any sign of action from the others in the tavern, Casca whispered to the man, "Just take it easy. My friend and I are not after your purse or your lives. But what in the name of Mithra has brought two such as yourselves to this place?" His mention of one of the favored gods of the legions brought a spark to the old man's eye.

"You're a Roman?" he queried. His voice, full and strong, had the air of a man who was used to being obeyed.

Casca poured his guest a portion of their beer from the clay pot container and replied, "Aye, I was born in Rome and served in her legions as a

common soldier. My name is Casca Longinus, and
my oversized friend here is Glam Tyrsbjorn." He
looked over the old man's face, which was intelligent and strong, though time had taken its toll.
There were scars on the face as well as the hands,
and Casca was sure there were more under his
robes. He'd been a warrior, and not a common
one, either. Here was a man of noble blood and
there was no way he could hide it, not even if he'd
been weighted down and carrying hod. There was
no way he could possibly have denied or hidden his
heritage. Casca continued, "And who, if I may ask,
are you, sir?"

The old warrior drew himself erect in his seat, his
body assuming the old habits of command and
birth. "I am Q. Iulianius Scaevola, and this young
man," indicating the boy, who was beginning to
nod his head, "is my ward." The warmth of the fire
after the cold outside was acting as an opiate for
his tired young body.

The old man's eyes rested questioningly on
Glam for a moment, but the barbarian's obvious
good humor and the fact that he'd cleared off a
bench so the boy could lie down and then had covered him with his own fur robe had eased the aged
one's mind.

Scaevola was no fool; he'd read the intent in the
faces of the other guests of the inn and knew full
well that the Roman and his friend had come to
their aid and saved them from a possible confrontation. For this reason, and because it was good to
speak Latin again, the old man felt inclined to relax
a bit. After a few mugs of mulled wine he was
speaking freely to Casca, something he would not
have ordinarily done, due to the obvious low birth

of the former legionary. But now he felt he owed
the man a debt and these were unusual circum-
stances. Scaevola had never been one to stand on
ceremony when it was uncalled for. They soon
began to talk, as all soldiers will and do. They
shared the common bindings of men who had lived
with violence but had not yet lost their own humanity. This made them comrades of the spirit, if
nothing else.

Glam had already followed the boy's lead. Without any comment he had laid his own shaggy head
on the wooden planks and had fallen into a noisy
slumber, leaving the two Romans free to talk.
Scaevola inquired of Casca as to the possibility of
obtaining private quarters for the night and was
told that it would probably be best for all of them
to stay the night there in the common room where
they could keep an eye on the other guests. From
what Glam had told him of this place, it was not
uncommon for a well-heeled guest to wake up in
the morning and find he'd been robbed, if he were
fortunate enough to make it to the morning alive.

Scaevola had been around in his time and agreed
with Casca's suggestion that they all stay where
they were near the fire and thus be able to take
turns watching while the others slept.

The night wore on and Scaevola trusted his in-
stincts. This place was on the Roman side of the
Rhine, near the mouth of the river that fed into the
sea, separating Gaul from Britannia, and the rule of
Rome was held thinly here. But there was something about his newfound companion that gave
him confidence in the man's integrity; and as the
wine loosened his tongue, so his story came forth.

Scaevola was a former praetor who'd made a

mistake. That mistake had been in being loyal to the man to whom he'd sworn allegiance as a judicial magistrate.

The last four years had been hard ones for the followers of Albinus. Lucius Septimus Severus, the African from Leptis Magna, was now master of the world. His legions had proclaimed him emperor after Iulianius had been murdered. But others too had put in their claim for the throne of Rome. Syria had proclaimed for Niger, and Britain had proclaimed for Albinus, but Severus had beaten them both to the Imperial City. After the death of Pertinax, Severus made a forced march to the gates of Rome. It had been said that not one soldier of his legion had removed even his breastplate between Carnuntum and Rome.

The praetorian guard had proclaimed Iulianius as emperor, but the real power of Rome rested with the legions, and they were outside the walls. The praetorians deserted their choice, and when they'd gone over to Severus, so had the senate. The pen may be mightier than the sword, but not when the sword's at your throat.

Iulianius had been murdered and later the praetorians were exiled to within a hundred miles of the city with the warning that if any should return they would be put to death. Severus had formed a new guard of his own men and the senate had confirmed his claim as emperor; but before July he'd had to leave for the east to deal with Niger. Three engagements had been fought, the last of which took place at Issus, where Niger had been killed. It had taken Severus another two years to pacify the regions of the east and in the process, he'd destroyed a good portion of Byzantium.

After that, he'd turned his attentions to the west and Albinus, who'd made Britain his stronghold and had strong forces to the north of Gaul.

Severus still needed the support of the senate, and had so far lived up to his bargain with them. None had been put to death and they blessed his achievements and gave him the laurels of conqueror and savior of the empire. With the support of the senate and fresh forces, he met Albinus on a plain to the north of Lyon between the Saone and the Rhone rivers.

The old man wiped a tear from his eye at the remembrance. "That," he continued, "was the worst conflict between Roman armies since the battle of Philippi." He swallowed a drink and continued.

"My Lord Albinus knew the battle was lost, and before the final blow was struck, he ordered me to leave the field and flee to Britain. I obeyed, and this," he indicated the sleeping boy, "is the reason. He is the natural son of Albinus and as such, is condemned to death. The mother, my own daughter, took her life at the news of Albinus' death. That is why we are here—to avoid the proscription that has come forth. Now that Severus has eliminated all his opposition, he has taken his mask off. In order to legitimize his succession, he has proclaimed that he is the son of Marcus Aurelius and the brother of Commodus."

He paused for a moment to catch his breath. The passion of his story was tiring him. "So far, Severus has put over sixty senators to death on charges of having sympathized with Albinus. I have come to this place with hopes for taking a ship to Spain. There I will find sanctuary for the son of Albinus, my grandson, among friends who will see that he is protected."

Weariness was overcoming the old man. Casca told him to rest and that he would watch over them this night. In the morning he would help them find a ship that would take them to Spain. He liked this aged gentleman and wished him well, but he feared that Rome was too powerful an enemy to leave alive anyone that might later have claim against the throne. The first law of power was to survive at any and all costs; and what was the value of one sleeping child against the glory of being known as the master of the world? Shaking his head sadly, he knew the answer: none! There was little chance that the boy would ever grow to manhood.

That night while the three others slept, Casca sat in the red glow of the fireplace and kept watch over the sleepers. One hand to his bared sword, he waited for the dawn and the passing of the winter storm. The others in the room did not miss the implications of the bared sword, and decided to leave the matter alone for the night.

One by one, all fell into their own state of sleep. The inn was silent, save for the crackling of the fire, which Casca replenished from time to time, and for the snoring of the men in their sleep. Several times Casca felt himself starting to doze off, but his head would jerk back up as if startled by something, and his eyes would come into instant focus.

He used old soldier's tricks to keep himself awake—breathing deeply to pump air into his lungs, standing for a while and stamping his feet, stretching his body—anything to keep his mind alert. For he knew that if he slept, there would be death in this room tonight; and he didn't care to experience that crap merely because he couldn't manage to stay awake for a few hours.

The boy snored softly in a child's slumber, and Casca pitied him. Through no fault of his own the youngster's was bound up in the fate of the empire and subject to its harsh laws. Casca knew from experience that fate was often cruel. Intellectually, he understood the laws of power and its survival. He knew some people felt that it would be better for all concerned that this single child should die now, for in later years he might prove to be the rallying figure that would bring thousands to their death in war uprisings. One small death in exchange for many?

The hours crept by until, instinctively, he knew the hour of daybreak was near.

Going from one to the other he shook his companions gently into awareness. The silence outside told them that the storm had passed over.

Waking the innkeeper, they settled their bill and bought a packet of food for each to take with him. Scaevola wrapped his grandson in the boy's cloak and took him by the hand as they left the smoky confines of the inn.

They walked through the narrow, icy streets; those streets were clean now, but with the coming of spring, the filth that lay below the blanket of virgin snow would come again into its own. Before leaving, Casca had looked over the men in the tavern and had waited until Scaevola and the child were safely outside with Glam before speaking. Softly, almost gently, he warned those awake and watching.

"If I see even one of you outside, you'll die. The old man and the boy are not for the likes of you.

Leave them alone or sing your death songs before leaving." The soft, deadly intent of the manner in which he spoke did more to convince the thieves and murderers present to let these easy pickings go. After all, there would be others; there was no rush. Time was always on the side of the killer, and they knew it.

The door closed behind him as he moved a little faster to catch up with Glam and the others, now heading for the river. There they contracted the services of a fisherman to take them downriver to the estuary where the old man and his ward could find a vessel to sail them to what was hoped would be the safety of far-off Spain.

As for Casca and Glam, the fisherman would set them on the other side of the river in Germania. He and Glam had had enough of civilization and now longed for the clean isolation of the primordial forests. At least there the dangers were clean, the men easy to understand, and the reasons for living and dying less complicated.

Scaevola held his grandson's left hand while the boy waved with his right a good-bye to the Roman and his hairy companion. Casca wished he could have done more for them. He liked the praetor, but he could detect the smell of a man already dead about him, and knew that there was nothing he could do about it. Each had to follow what Glam called his "weird," and reach his own destiny, wherever it might be. As for the boy, Casca merely sighed and his head felt a little heavier. The circle turns; it has happened before and it shall happen again: one small life for many.

Ambition is the greatest disease and killer of man that the world has ever known. More than any plague, man's desire to inflict his will on others has caused the senseless deaths of millions, and to what end? All kings must die. What then have they accomplished with their ambition and self-delusion of power? For their lives are nothing more than fleeting moments in the course of centuries, and don't really matter all that much.

Glam broke trail into a line of pines that marked the end of the world, at least as Rome knew it. They were back in his lands now and he was content. He breathed in deeply the crisp, clean air and kicked up a flurry of snow from a covered bush.

"Hey there, you Dago titmouse," Glam called out, "knock off the long face. Everything awaits us. Somewhere out there." He indicated the deep woods, pointing. "Yes, my friend, somewhere out there lies adventures for us and a good clean warrior's life. Don't worry about the old man; he'll do all right for himself and the boy. And if he doesn't, he's only living the life that the gods have ordained—so why fight it?" He urged Casca on, "Come on, you Latin castratto, or I'll beat you to the women."

Casca laughed, the tension of the previous night broken by the good-naturedness of Glam. "What women, you great hirsute mongrel?"

Glam shrugged. "How should I know? But somewhere there are always women; we just have to find them, that's all."

The trees closed around them, and once more the Rhine was left behind them.

Chapter Five

The two men stood, dark figures in stark contrast to the blinding white of the snow-covered fields and valleys below. From their aerie in the heights, overlooking the sheltered valley, they watched with wary eyes.

The ice wind from the sea, racing in from the frozen waters to the far north, whipped at their fur robes and leggings. Both men wore beards and mustaches. What skin was exposed was darkened from the months of exposure to the elements. Wisps of frozen breath rose from their mouths and nostrils, small steaming clouds of vapor that rapidly disappeared in the gusting winds of the Nordic winter. On the horizon, dark clouds were gathering to once again assault the rocky crags and valleys with new waves of snow and ice.

Casca pointed to the stone buildings below, his words punctuated by renewed bursts of frozen breath. "Do we go down?"

His companion grunted, as was his habit, in the affirmative. "Aye, we don't have much choice in the matter. There's nothing behind us but that which we have left—endless woods and starvation. And I'm hungry enough now to consider boiling down my own furs for supper."

The thought of Glam trying to digest his own louse- and flea-infested robes brought the beginning of a smile to him, but it passed as rapidly as it had come. "I don't know. From what I've heard, the old bastard that rules here at Helsfjord is not the most gracious of hosts."

Glam nodded. "Aye, but still one thing he has to do is honor the laws of hospitality. Anyone from outside his lands who claims shelter before he can kill or declare them enemies must be given three days of shelter before he has to leave. In that time, the master of the hold may not give him injury without just cause."

Casca responded, "And just what might those below consider *just cause?*"

Glam reflected a moment. "Almost anything that would remotely resemble an affront to his honor. If we go down there, we'll have to walk slowly and speak carefully. These weapons of ours, made of good steel, are wealth enough for Ragnar to have us killed or fed to the crabs at the tide stakes."

Casca eyed the walls of the hold, built with native stones quarried from the sides of the surrounding fjord. Smoke rose from several fires and chimneys and in his mind, even from this distance, he thought he could smell the odors of roasting meat. They had had none in the last four days since they had killed and eaten their last horse, a bad-tempered semiswaybacked beast that tried more often than not to take a plug out of Casca when he came too close. Casca enjoyed the thought that he had at least had the last bite where the foul-minded beast was concerned. It had been tough and

stringy, with too little fat on it to give a man
strength. True, the soup they had made from the
marrowbones had been satisfying, but with Glam
at the table, there wouldn't have been much left
after one or two feedings even if they had been eating an elephant.

Glam put his long, double-bladed, two-handed
sword back into its sling on his back and hitched
the battle axe, hanging from a thong at his waist, a
little higher.

"Well then, if it's settled, my little Dago titmouse, we might as well get our asses down there
and see what kind of greeting we'll get at the gate."

Casca shifted his pack up on his shoulders a little
higher, bitching at the weight, and Glam responded with a lack of understanding as to why
Casca hadn't long since sold the contents. He could
see no good reason for the Roman to hold onto the
legionnaires breastplate of boiled leather with
heavy iron rings sewn to it. True, it had come in
handy a time or two when they had pawned it for
enough copper or silver to see them through until
they could get their hands on some money or find
a job. But the Roman always went back for it.
Why?

Casca said nothing about his reasons, though he
sometimes questioned himself about his holding
onto the armor. Perhaps it gave him a sense of
identity that he needed from time to time. The legion, for all its faults, had been the only home he
had ever known. It was where he had grown into
manhood, those years when his personality had
been formed. No matter how far away from the
legion he might run or for how many years or even
centuries, it was the same for him as for other men

who were raised in a settled home with family. You could never completely lose them. In the remote recesses of the mind, home would always be with you, and the legion was his home.

Stumbling and sliding, they worked their way down through thigh-deep drifts of snow, tripping and falling over hidden roots and limbs, then rising only to slip and fall again. When they reached the last fifty feet, they just gave up, picked out a long, icy slide, and, like children, sped down the last of the climb to the bottom of the valley floor on their butts.

Working their way through the drifts, they finally reached the gray walls of Helsfjord. Their lungs were aching from the cold. Ice, frozen on their beards, gave them a look of frozen corpses lately risen from some frigid grave.

Their labored breathing from their exertions spoke of life, though, and the red blotchy patches on their cheeks showed that warm red blood still coursed through their veins. Even now, that slight sign of color was fading back into pale gray patches as they caught their breath and began to breathe more easily.

A head above them peered out over the rampart. The head was covered with the fur of a muskrat turned inside out to put the fur next to the skin. A dirty face with watery eyes and grimy skin spoke. "Who is it? What do you want at the gates of Ragnar of Helsfjord?"

Glam spoke first, quick to give the man on the rampart no chance to say anything else. "Two travelers who claim the ancient right of hospitality."

The man on the wall groaned, knowing he had been outsmarted, which, to be honest about it, had never been particularly hard for anyone to accomplish. His ass would be in trouble now. Again he called down to the two men waiting for the doors of the hold to open and admit them. "Who are you that cry for the mercy of Ragnar? Are you beggars that you come pleading at his door?"

Casca started to respond angrily, but a touch from Glam's paw restrained him as he whispered in Casca's ear, "Don't screw things up now. We got him where we want him and he's just trying to get us pissed off enough to say or do something stupid so they can deny us shelter. Remember, just take it easy and we'll have at least three days in which to warm our bones before they can throw us out."

Glam repeated his request in gentle, well-mannered words. The face above, knowing he had been outwitted, did what all underlings do—he called for his superior. "You two wait there," he shouted, and disappeared from sight behind the gray stones of the wall.

A few minutes passed, which Glam and Casca spent stamping their feet and slapping their arms against each other to pound some warmth into their bodies. A few flakes of fresh, clean snow were beginning to fall.

A new voice spoke to them from the wall. The face that went with it was much neater than the other. He repeated the same questions and received the same answers. He scratched his chin and lowered his voice. "Would you fellows like a little advice?" Not waiting for a response, he continued. "It would perhaps be better if you didn't claim the rights of hospitality and went on about your business. You might find the weather outside not to be as cold as the reception you'd receive behind these walls. This is a stern household and doesn't make many welcome."

Casca had made note of the cleanliness of this man's appearance in contrast to the underling they had first spoken to. For, over the years he had come to realize that a man who took care of his appearance and body usually had more brains than those who didn't. Casca wanted to respond to this fellow. "We still claim the rights, warrior, though we give you thanks for your advice. But we would not willingly spend another night in the open, especially with a new storm brewing on the horizon."

The watcher on the ramparts glanced behind him at the gathering darkness of rushing clouds, which spoke of a major storm's approach. Looking back down, he said, "Well, I can't say I really blame you for that, and if you're determined to enter, then lay aside your weapons at the portal before entering and the gate will be opened. Remember, no weapons allowed inside, and that includes your eating knives. I'll meet you at the entrance."

Casca called before the man could leave. "And what is your name warrior? I would know so that one day perhaps I will be able to repay you for your courtesy."

The man looked back down, clear blue eyes set over a strong nose. "I am Sifrit, son of Olaf Scarbrow."

Glam and Casca moved to the door, where a small window in the gate opened for them to hand over their weapons. Casca was still reluctant, but Glam assured him that they would be returned when they left, providing they were still alive and able to leave.

Once the handing-over was accomplished, they were admitted entry through a creaking wooden door that showed a dire need of having its hinges, which were of hammered native bronze, oiled.

The man called Sifrit gave them a quick search for any hidden weapons and motioned for them to follow. Casca liked the looks of the man— medium-height with wide shoulders and narrow hips that rode on strong, muscled legs. A sword of fair steel rode in a homemade leather scabbard at his side.

The gate closed behind them.

Chapter Six

Sifrit escorted the weary travelers into the central structure of the hold down a narrow corridor with a strong door at each end and a walkway at the top from which attackers could be ambushed if they got this far into the fort. Casca wrinkled his nose. After weeks in the open air of the forests, the smell of the hall assaulted his nostrils. Ragnar evidently was not one much concerned with hygiene. The straw on the floor of the hallway was at least a year old and the spongy feel of it under his leather sandals said there were several more layers covered up under the latest batch of decaying straw. Sifrit hesitated a moment before showing them through the last door leading to the Great Room, which the feasting hall and common room were called.

Speaking softly Sifrit said, "Listen, you guys. I don't know anything about you, but I do know that if you give the master any excuse at all to claim you have broken faith so he can call off the laws of hospitality, he will. And neither one of you will see daylight again. I take that back. It's not often that he uses the dungeon below, as he's too cheap to waste even leftovers on someone who doesn't show him a profit. More than likely you'll end up on the crab stakes in the fjord."

Glam shuddered at the words "crab stakes." Casca, confused, asked what Sifrit meant by that, and Glam told him. It was common punishment for crimes ranging from short-changing the chief to treason. They would tie you to a wooden stake at low tide, and when the waters came back in, so did the crabs. They would eat the unfortunate person on the stakes inch by inch. Quite often, all that was left when the waters again receded would be the victim's head. They were always very careful to place the stakes far enough up on the beach so the victim would not be given the mercy of drowning if he lived long enough for the waters to reach that high.

Casca understood the shudder and gave one himself. "And they thought that being crucified was rough!"

Sifrit continued. "The only thing that might help you is to claim to be mercenaries and in exchange for hospitality, you'll give him the service of your blades. But watch him. He might put you to the test."

Casca and Glam both nodded their understanding and followed him into the Great Hall. It may have been great by the standards of the northlands, perhaps, but it was a poor place of ruling by any civilized standards. Ragnar had certainly never seen the Palace of Imperial Nero or even the Asian Despot, Herod.

The floors were even filthier than in the hallway and stank with the sour-sweet odor of decayed meat. The source of the odor was evident from the number of chewed bones on the floor. These locals had the habit of tossing anything they didn't consume onto the floor for the dogs to fight over. The walls were spotted here and there with some lonely trophies—a few spears and leather-covered shields and a couple of tapestries that had seen much better days. But still, they served to give a little color to the otherwise drab and gray surroundings. A roaring fire in a hearth, large enough to roast an entire ox in, gave out the only source of warmth. Narrow, open slits set high in the walls let in some air and also let out some of the smoke from the fire, half of which seemed to find its way into the room and not up the chimney.

The master of Helsfjord was easy enough to spot. He was the biggest and meanest bastard sitting at the oaken table, stuffing his face with roast pork still steaming from the fire. The juices from the half-cooked flesh were dripping down his mouth into his beard. On either side sat a half dozen of his senior warriors; they were all hard-looking men with the scars of battle on them and the look of killers in their eyes.

Ragnar farted and wiped his fingers on his beard and in his gray hair, making sure that he paid special attention to his bald spot, for he knew, as all did, that pig fat was good for growing new hair. The significance of fact that he had been smearing his balding patch with the stuff for fifteen years with no noticeable results never occurred to him.

Ragnar squinted at them, one eye screwed up as if trying to focus. "Well," he grunted, "what do you want here?"

Sifrit explained that they claimed hospitality. Ragnar stroked his white-streaked dirty beard with even dirtier fingers. Grudgingly he knew he had to give in. One day he might have to make such claim himself, and if he ever refused it to anyone, it would never be granted to him. The law was the law. "Well then, you have three days and then you get your asses out of my house. I'll feed no useless mouths here."

Casca sized the man up. Anyone that disagreeable was bound to have more than his fair share of enemies. "Lord Ragnar, if you would grant us permission to winter in your lands, we would pay you back with the aid of our arms, should anyone come to attack you."

Ragnar thought it over. He had always been a little short of manpower. As soon as his young men got their size on them, they headed for better paying hunting grounds. Ungrateful bastards! And these two did have the look of experienced fighters about them, though he didn't like the looks of the smaller man. He was far too clean in appearance— like that fop, Sifrit. But no matter. If he could get them cheap enough, he might make them a deal. And anyway, it was always possible for them to break some of the laws, and if they didn't break any, it could always be arranged so it looked that way.

Slyly, he forced a little good humor into his voice, though it fooled no one, not even himself. "Well then, that's a different matter. Anyone will tell you that old Ragnar is a fair man to anyone who wants honest work and is willing to give fair exchange. Tell you what I'll do. You can winter here and we'll see how it works out. I'll supply your food and drink and if you work out all right, there'll be something to put in your purses when the spring comes. Now, what could be fairer than that?"

Glam looked at Casca. They read each other the same and agreed to the old bandit's terms.

They were shown to the bachelor males' barracks. They were to share a straw, thatch-covered, stone shelter with another twenty or so regulars that rotated their duty time with the other young men of the region over whom Ragnar ruled. Each pulled a short-timer hitch of sixty days and returned to his farm as another took his place. This was as according to custom, and they knew no other way. Like it or not, they owed Ragnar fealty and were made to swear a blood oath as soon as they were old enough to have pubic hair.

The next few days were spent as they always are when settling into new surroundings. There are always some young bucks who want to flex their muscles and make brave noises; and, as with children, this is usually all it comes to. The ones to watch were the older warriors with the look of bitterness in their eyes. After Glam and Casca had proved to everyone's satisfaction that they were not to be screwed around with, they were left pretty much to themselves.

Also, as was normal for new men, they drew the worst of the duty assignments: the late watches on the ramparts, going out on the wood-cutting details in the day, and anything else the senior warriors could think of to lay on them. All this, Casca and Glam tolerated. The winter was still too far from being over, so they swallowed their anger and accepted it.

Casca did find one person of interest, though

thus far he had had no chance to talk to her. She
was Lida, the daughter of Ragnar. He wondered
how such a foul brute could have sired anything so
graceful and delicate. Her hair was pale as winter
moonbeams and her skin almost transparent. It
was said, though not loudly, that Ragnar had
beaten her mother's brains out while in one of his
drunken rages, and most felt that was the easy way
out for her. But Lida he kept near him. Though she
was of age to marry and several times he had tried
to trade her off for a favorable alliance among
neighboring tribes, he could find no takers. None
wanted to claim Ragnar for a kinsman, no matter
how pretty his daughter was.

From what Casca had been able to find out, she
was nearly twenty years old and could even read.
This was something extremely rare in these parts,
where only the few druids he'd met in his travels
had any knowledge of writing, and that was in their
own manner. They used a system of squiggles and
marks that made no sense to him whatsoever. But
then, who said it had to? Her being able to read
and write gave her some value to Ragnar in keeping records of who owed him what—though sometimes she pissed him off when she pointed out that
someone he had a hard-on for owed him nothing.

Chapter Seven

Lida had noticed the scar-faced stranger with his broad shoulders and strong back. She also noticed how he never used his strength to hurt anyone lesser than himself. The children, too, seemed to like the rough man and often came to play with him or watch him twist pieces of iron into different shapes for their amusement and then straighten them out again. Several times they'd met by accident on the beaches where he would be helping the men on the fishing boats or when he stood guard at night on the ramparts. He was always courteous and somewhat distant, as if afraid of frightening her; perhaps he was afraid of her. Yes, that was it! He was afraid of her!

Lida decided that it was time for her to take action.

One midsummer's evening, when the heat of the night was on them and men and women tossed restlessly in their sleep, Casca walked the guard mount, his shield on his shoulder and spear in hand, staring out into the darkness. A whisper of bare feet brought his head around.

"Good evening, my lady."

Lida stood pale and wraithlike in the dark, lit by

the flames of a flickering torch set on the stairs
leading to the inner courtyard.

"It's late and I think it would be best if you
didn't wander about. Who knows what might happen?"

Lida had waited long enough, and that day
Glam had told her of his friend's feelings. And as
women often must, she decided to make up his
mind for him.

"Casca," her voice touched him. "Do you love
me?" The question made him lose his power of
speech and he stood mute. Lida stamped her bare
foot on the stones of the walkway. "Well, don't
just stand there with your mouth hanging open.
Answer me. . . . Do you love me?"

Casca cleared his throat and managed to croak
out, "I do."

Lida took a deep breath. "Good, then that's settled. Now, what are we going to do about it? I love
you, too, and I'm going to have you for my husband." Casca was now completely confused.

At night on his pallet, he had been seeing her
form in his dreams, walking gracefully, her pale
hair let loose and flowing with the wind. She had
been constantly in his thoughts and he *was* afraid
that he was falling in love with her. Glam hadn't
failed to notice the reason for Casca's distractions,
which came only when the Lady Lida was about,
and he had decided that in order to get his friend's
mind back on business, it would be a good thing
for him to play matchmaker. As the two were obviously in love with each other, he'd thought he
would just help them achieve what they both really
wanted.

When the Lady Lida was about, Glam had managed to arrange for Casca to be nearby too, and it had tickled him to see the only man he'd ever met that could whip his ass in a hand-to-hand fight act like a love-struck cow.

And Casca had finally admitted to himself that all along she had been the reason that he had talked Glam into hanging around long after the snows were gone. He had known it was wrong for him to stay, but he couldn't help it, and every day he had fallen deeper in love and tried to justify it. After all, wasn't he entitled to a little bit of happiness? Was it asking too much to be allowed to love someone? In his heart he knew the answers to both questions, and pushed them deliberately from his mind.

So now they found ways to be together, to meet while he was on guard duty, a touch of the hand when passing. Only Glam and Sifrit knew what was happening, and Sifrit tried to warn Casca away from the path he was following. If Ragnar were to find out, there was no telling what he might do.

Another pair of eyes were watching, too—sharper eyes than those of old Ragnar. They belonged to the druid priest, Hagdrall. He was a bitter old man with a gray beard, wrinkled skin, and the eyes of one filled with unrealized ambitions.

Hagdrall served as the teacher and counselor of the hold. He would cast the spells that told of the future and that supposedly brought luck. In the spring he supervised the sacrifice of virginal children to Mother Earth so that the crops would grow. He also sold bags of wind to those who went out on the fishing boats. If one of the bags had no wind in it and the fisherman complained, Hagdrall always blamed it on the purchaser's careless handling of the bag, and that he'd foolishly let the wind escape.

His eyes missed little, and he knew the signs of love. The way that Lida walked, with the new spring to her step and the way she held her head a little higher, the glow in her cheeks, and her laughter all served to tell the druid that there was a man in her life. It didn't take him long to find out who it was, and the news pleased him. He didn't like anyone who refused to acknowledge his powers, and this foreign warrior was dangerous to him because he had done just that. Even old Ragnar was careful of the priest and his spells.

Several times in the past, men and women alike had died when they'd gotten on the bad side of Hagdrall. He'd put the evil eye on them, making his magical signs that brought forth the elemental spirits of the underworld to do his bidding. He always covered up the work of his poisons with a little sideshow display that took the watchers attention away from his quick hands.

It was he who counseled Ragnar and it was through him that Ragnar's brothers in Britannia had agreed to arrange a royal wedding between Lida and Icenius, the descendent and heir apparent of the warrior queen, Bodaciea. The youngster needed a place to quarter and try to rebuild his forces for a new war against Rome.

The druids were picking this time to make a try for power because of the internal difficulties present in Rome and on her frontiers. They claimed young Icenius was the direct descendent of the Queen of the Iceni, who had destroyed over seventy thousand Romans and their allies some

150 years ago. Even the boy didn't know any different.

The druids had taken him as a boy and raised him. He knew only what they had told him. His kingdom was small. It consisted of a few villages among the Scoti of Caledonia, to the north but well beyond the reach of the Pax Romana.

Icenius was unaware that when his usefulness to the druids was over, he was expendable. He would live only while they had a use for him. All other offers for an alliance with him had been refused. Ragnar was their last hope. If that fell through, the boy would die.

The druids of Britannia had sung the praises of Ragnar in his ear and thought that if Icenius left Britannia for the northlands, he would be able to rally forces there, using the strength of his mother's name and Ragnar's hold as an operational base. The fact that they'd told him of the beauty of Ragnar's daughter had also helped some.

Messengers between the two parties finally arrived at an agreement concerning the dowery, and the marriage was agreed upon. For old Ragnar's part, because of the youth of the princeling, he figured he ought to be able to control the youngster, and he himself would be the power behind the throne, that was, if the boy was successful in his attempt to regain the crown of his great-grandmother.

But if he married the Lady Lida and failed, still Ragnar was out very little. But . . . if the young prince won and by chance put a child into Lida's belly, and should then suffer a . . . fatal accident, say, then the daughter of Ragnar would be queen. And that was almost as good as if he wore the crown himself. All these possibilities had been carefully explained to Ragnar by Hagdrall.

On the day Ragnar was to make the announcement of his daughter's upcoming nuptials, Hagdrall whispered in his ear of her relationship with the Roman. Hagdrall was sore put to restrain Ragnar from arresting Casca and having him put to the stakes at once. Ragnar finally agreed with him that it would be better to make an example of the Roman at the announcement ceremony, and . . . it would please his new allies to have him deliver justice to one of their hated enemies.

Ragnar gave the orders to several of his most trusted henchmen: bring Casca to him in chains that night at the feast and keep it a secret until then. No one was to know. He sent Glam and Sifrit out to the countryside on an errand that would occupy them for a couple of days. Ostensibly, they were to gather up some oxen that were owed to him on a debt and bring them back to Helsfjord. By the time they returned, it would all be over. Hagdrall had convinced Ragnar it would be better not to kill or punish the two Nordics if he could possibly avoid it. They had too many friends, especially Sifrit and his family, who were well connected with several other tribes. By the time they returned, justice would be done within the laws of the tribes and there would be nothing Glam or Sifrit could do but accept it. However, if they were there when Casca was taken, they might fight for him and that could lead to a blood feud that would defeat their purpose.

After Sifrit and Glam had left on their errand, Casca was summoned to the storerooms and was told that he would be picking up a new issue of clothing for himself and Glam as a reward for their good services.

When he got there, the lights went out and three men jumped him and clubbed him down to his knees, quickly locking him in arm and leg irons. He was kept there until the time came for him to be brought before Ragnar for sentencing.

Guests began to arrive with the setting of the sun. They had received invitations to attend the gathering, having been told only that it was for a great purpose. Not even Lida knew the true reason for the gathering, and when the opening toast and wassail was made, she sat as usual at her place next to her father. Ragnar waited until his guests had eaten and drunk enough to put them in good humor. They were well pleased at the amounts of food and drink Ragnar had set his table with. It was far better than anything the cheap old bastard had laid out before.

Ragnar finished stuffing his face with roast duck and venison, wiped his hands on his beard and bald spot, and stood. Hammering his fist on the table, he called out for the attention of his guests.

"Welcome and wassail, friends and neighbors. . . . I have invited you here this day for two reasons. One is an occasion of celebration, the other to see justice done." Silence settled over the crowd. They knew the temper of Ragnar's justice and pitied the poor wretch, whoever he might be. Ragnar cleared his throat and spat a hunk of phlegm to the straw-covered floor. "On this day I announce the marriage of my daughter, Lida, to Icenius of Britannia."

Lida said nothing; she was stunned. Only the draining of blood from her face told that she had heard her father's announcement.

"The other is to see a spy punished. Bring in the dog," he roared. The doors to the Hall opened and Casca was kicked and dragged into the center of the room.

Pointing a dirty finger at the Roman, Ragnar proclaimed, "This dog here, who has eaten at my table and claimed the laws of hospitality, is a spy for Rome. He knew of the talks between my emissaries and those of Icenius, and has tried to subvert the alliance by disaffecting the loyalties of my daughter, turning her young head with smooth words and lies. Only the sharp eyes of the druid, Hagdrall, have prevented him from being successful in completing his plan to kidnap my child and take her to the slave pens of Rome." He called upon the priest to stand.

Hagdrall did so.

"Is this not true, priest?"

Hagdrall drew his scrawny frame up as erectly as he could and raised his staff. "By the Holy Oak and Sacred Tree of Life, I so swear."

An angry murmur ran through the listeners. Ragnar took a deep pull at a horn of beer and continued. "Then, if no one can offer defense in this dog's favor, I will give judgment."

None did. Lida's attempt to rise was halted by the grip of the druid's hand over her mouth.

"I sentence you, spy of Rome, to the tide stakes!"

Lida bit through the druid's fingers, almost taking off the little one. The priest hopped about, holding his hand and cursing. Lida stood. Her face regaining its color, she faced her father. "He lies and you lie. Casca is no spy. He is my lover."

Ragnar was astounded. His daughter had never

stood up to him before.

He roared for her to be silent, anger building at the edges of his mind, his eyes narrowing. The bitch was just like her mother, ungrateful.

Lida stood her ground. "You lie and this filthy old faker lies and you know it. I will not marry Icenius."

Ragnar was losing control.

"You will do as I say." His eyes had turned red and his hand trembled with barely controlled rage. The guests began to move back to put some distance between them and Ragnar. They had seen him go into one of his rages before.

Lida screamed at him, "I will not obey. . . . I will have no other man for my husband. . . . You may kill me as you did my mother, but you can't make me take another to my bed. I have eyes for Casca and none other."

Ragnar broke, froth foaming at his mouth and staining his beard. He moved to face his child. His hand reached out and took a burning brand from its iron wall socket and held it above his head.

"What did you say?"

Lida repeated her words. "I have eyes for none but Casca."

Ragnar thrust the burning torch straight into her face. With his other hand, he held her steady as she screamed under the flames. Ragnar laughed an insane cackle. "Then by all the gods, you will have your wish and have no eyes." He released her to fall on the floor in a faint. The smell of burnt hair and scorched flesh floated through the Hall.

Casca howled and tried to lunge forward, only to be beaten unconscious by the clubs of his guards.

The guests were silent and slowly began to leave,

until only Ragnar sat at his table, breathing heavily, eyes red-rimmed, and mad, cursing to himself as he had done when he'd smashed the brains out of Lida's mother.

Even Hagdrall left. There was no dealing with Ragnar when he was like this. But the brute had screwed up his deal with the druids of Britannia. The prince would not take a compromised woman, especially a blind one.

Lida's housemaids carried her to her room and put warm poultices of herbs and saltwater on her burns to help heal the blisters on her face. These would fade with time, but when she opened her eyes, they would be only clear milky orbs looking out at nothing. She was blind and would be until the day she died.

Casca came to, his head feeling as if it were trying to burst from the inside out. He tried to move his hands, but couldn't. Slowly, the realization of his predicament came to him as the smell of the sea hit his nostrils. He was chained to a tidal stake. He was completely alone, just him and the waters a few feet away. The tide was coming in and with it would come the flesh-eating crabs with pincers and their hungry, constantly opening-and-closing mouths.

Thoughts of Lida plagued him. Those and his hatred for Ragnar were of more concern to him than the approaching waters that now tickled the toes of his feet and rushed back, only to come again, each time a little higher.

He wondered when the crabs would come and how long it would take for them to tear him apart, one tiny nip at a time. Even more important was, would he die if they did dismantle him?

How powerful was the curse of life put on him
by the crucified Jew? He had received wounds that
should have killed but yet, he lived. When he'd
tried to commit suicide outside Ctesiphon, death
had again been denied him. But what would happen now?

There was nothing he could do but wait. He
knew the answer to his questions would not be long
in coming. The water had reached his waist and he
felt the small things of the sea slithering and crawling over his feet and legs. The water was reaching
his chest and waves were lapping up to touch his
chin. The worst was the cold, which numbed the
body and brain.

Then he felt the first tentative nips at his flesh.
The crabs were there. He felt a large one crawl over
his bare feet then another using his claws to creep
up his thigh to his waist. One sting, then another,
and another. He knew he was bleeding into the water, tiny rivers of blood from a dozen pincer cuts.
He waited for the rest of the crabs to come in, for
they would come in dozens and even hundreds to
pick his bones clean. The waiting was the worst
part, but the crabs did finally come. Like herds of
lice they swarmed over his body, each taking one
tiny bite and no more.

And then, as blood stained more of the water
surrounding him, the crabs began to leave, as did
the small fish that had come with them to claim
what scraps they could. They went back to their
holes in the crevices and rocks of the fjord. There
was something about the man on the stake that
wasn't to their liking. The fish kept their distance,
too. The scent of his blood served as a shield to
ward off even a cruising shark, who opened his

gapped, thousand-fanged mouth, took one taste of the blood, and fled back to deep water. This one was not to be touched. The cold and fatigue took him, and his head nodded down as darkness wrapped itself about him.

When the tide receded, a curious warrior from the hold came to inspect the remains, took one look and yelling, ran back to the fort. Soon, others came to see if what the warrior had said was true. A crowd gathered on the stones of the beach and waited. They did not know why. They only knew that something had happened that had never occurred before. The murmurs brought Ragnar and the druid to the scene.

Casca's body was covered with hundreds of tiny bites, but that was all. No bones showed through his rib cage. The Roman survived.

The druid made signs to ward off evil and Ragnar chewed his beard in confusion. Making up his mind, Ragnar called to a couple of his spearmen. "If the crabs won't have him then you finish him off. Use him for target practice."

But at this, Hagdrall had to interfere. In his own way, he believed in magic and spirits and the curses that could come if the laws were broken. Raising his staff, he stopped the spearmen. "No! Ragnar. The law says that any who survive the tide stakes may not be killed."

Ragnar thought about the situation for a few moments, then made up his mind. "All right, if that's the way of it, then I won't do him any harm at all." He laughed a nasty sound. "By Wotan, I won't lay a hand on him." Motioning to his spearmen, he said, "Take him to the dungeons and leave him there. No one is to ever enter his cell and

he is not to be given food or drink. If I can't kill
him then I'll just let him do it for me. After all, I
can't be held responsible if he starves to death, now
can I?"

Casca heard his sentence and tried to speak, but
dropped back off into the darkness.

Chapter Eight

Consciousness slowly crept back to him. The throbbing in his head threatened to keep the darkness with him. Filth from the straw-covered stone floor filled his mouth with a bitter taste. He rose to all fours, shaking his head to clear it of the cobwebs trying to drag him down.

Slowly, painfully, he forced his eyes open, only to see black. The dungeon was as dark as his thoughts. He dragged himself to the side of the wall, feeling his way with blind hands. Slowly, bitterly, full awareness came to him.

Remembrance. . . !

Rising, he stood in the dark and screamed, "Lida . . ." Even from the depths of the underground chambers, his cry could be heard faintly in the halls above: "Lida. . . ." Battle-toughened veterans shivered and made the two-finger sign to ward off evil spirits.

After a time, he grew used to the darkness. There was a thin blue-tinged glow in the cell where a minute amount of light came in from a single narrow slit, high on the wall. There was nothing in the cell—no cot or pallet, no blankets or anything to cover his nakedness with. There was only the filth-encrusted straw, which he knew from the sour odor of urine hadn't been changed in years. Going through the straw, he found a single wooden bowl; though from what Ragnar had said, he would never have food in it.

He was to starve. Hate settled on him, forcing the pain from his mind, taking him over with one thought and goal. One day he would come out of this crypt. Those above would think him dead soon and, though it might be years, he would be silent. There would be no sound from him to tell Ragnar he lived; and one day that door would open and when it did, the Hall above would run red with rivers of blood. He would take his vengeance then.

He was used to going days without food, but the lack of water was unbearable. There was nothing, not even a drop of moisture to dampen his lips with. It was three days before he discovered the dung beetles living beneath the decaying layers of packed straw on the floor. Each beetle had a tiny bit of moisture in its body.

It was a hunt. Casca would lie on his belly, fingers groping through the refuse, until he would feel the cool, hard shell of one of the insects. At first, he would pop them into his mouth as quickly as he found them, but he found later it was more satisfying to wait until he had a handful. Then he could taste the moisture. After chewing slowly, he would swallow them, shells and all; anything to fill the void in his gut.

Days became weeks and the weeks changed into seasons, and still Casca endured. He cursed himself for taking so long to discover that there was moisture to be had on the stone walls of his cell. There lingered cool beads that collected on the stones when the mist came in from the sea.

During the winter, he found warmth by crawling under the layers of impacted straw and lay there for days, forgetting even to lick the dew from the walls or eat his ration of beetles. Nearly comatose, he rested in a form not dissimilar from the hibernating animals of the forests. In the first months, he had several times thought he could never endure the idea of years of confinement in this one dark silent cell without going mad. It was worse than when he had been a slave in the mines of Greece. At least there he had work. It was something to do besides sit and watch the passing of light to dark from the single aperture cut in the wall, the only access to fresh air and mist from the fjord. It was too narrow for him to climb through and too high to reach. He lay there for days, watching the change from thin light to blackest dark, one cycle after another. He learned to turn his mind back on itself. To take a thought, isolate it, turn it around, and look at it from a thousand angles.

His beard grew, as did his nails. The beard, he did nothing about. At least it gave him some covering. His nails he chewed off and ate. Never was a word spoken to him. In obedience to Ragnar's orders, there were no visitors allowed. Not once did he even hear anyone pass by his cell. He knew they believed him dead by now—long dead, and no more than a shriveled husk lying withered in some corner, falling apart one joint at a time. Increasingly, he turned in on himself. Several times it was as if his soul had left his body and would float above the floor. He could look down, out of the spirit's eyes, and see himself in startling clarity. He saw filthy matted hair and beard, and ribs sticking out from the chest as if they were embarrassed to be of this body and wanted to find a new home.

He wished now he had listened to the words of Shiu, the yellow sage from far Khitai, a little more closely. The yellow man would have had no problem dealing with the isolation. He knew how to use his inner consciousness to live inside himself. He'd often said that that was all one really had to begin with and all that one would have to end this plane of existence with. The circle was always complete. One had merely to accept the idea that the mind was *all*. Time and the body were nothing. Desire was the singlemost item which caused all of man's grief and pain: the desire for wealth or power; or to have a horse, or to eat better food. Once man had rid himself of all physical desire, then he would find peace and be able to develop the only thing of true value . . . the mind. Man's only true purpose for existence was to think; for in the mind were found the answers to all questions and time was meaningless. If in one's life a man can but find one truth, and pass it on to those who come after him, he has done well.

But Casca was no philosopher, and try as he might to find the peaceful state of mind that Shiu counseled, it was hate that sustained him. The desire to have Ragnar's throat between his fingers was food for his soul; and the hope of vengeance satisfied him more than a handful of grub could ever do.

The only sounds he had ever heard were those faint trickles that crept through the aperture, distant and far. He had never made a sound. Not a word had come from his lips in two years, for he had a sense that told him it had been about that long. The corridor, connecting his cell to the rest of the dungeon, was similarly as quiet. He rested on the floor, his head lying on his forearm, facedown. His body was only half the weight it had been before his confinement, and most of that was from his bones. The elbows, knees, and wrists were swollen to twice their normal size, but it was only the shrinkage of the tissue around them that made them appear so large and deformed. His cheeks were drawn into the sides of his face, eyes sunken into deep hollows, hair hanging to his shoulders in dirty clotted Medusa tendrils, matted and held together from the two years of accumulated filth and body grime.

But he knew he would not die, and for once that pleased him. He would survive. He didn't understand or even care about the mechanics of his survival or how his body made the most of every atom of nourishment he consumed. He hadn't had a bowel movement since he had come there. A small blessing—at least he didn't have to add his own waste to the stink already present.

One thing he hadn't lost was all of his strength. What was left of him was twisted, knotted sinew and stringy muscle tissue. Most of every waking moment he exercised to keep away the weakness that would come if he merely stood idle, waiting. He knew he would one day have need for every ounce of strength he could muster.

The creaking of rusty hinges, followed by the thump of a door closing, made him jerk his head up from his arm. Rising, he stood beside the door. He waited, holding his breath, his heart pounding in his chest. Was this the day? Were they going to open the cell? Gruff voices, amused, came to him.

Two warriors were laughing at the sound of someone's misery. He could hear the sound of a man being dragged down the stone corridor. He almost bit through his lower lip in anticipation. They *must* open this cell. They had others, but this *must* be the one. If they passed by this time, when would he have another chance? It might not come again for years. They were near. It sounded like they were going to pass him by. He ran a dry tongue over his lips and gave a slow, soft whistle, once, then again. On the other side of the door, he could hear that the dragging sounds had stopped. Good, they were listening. He whistled again, slightly louder—just a strange, whispering trill.

The men on the other side cocked their ears at the sound. There were no prisoners in this corridor, unless someone had been moved without their knowledge, and that was unlikely.

One guard said to the other, "Isn't this the cell where Ragnar put the Roman?"

His associate responded in the affirmative. "Aye, but that was two or more years ago, and as you well know he was to starve. There has been no one permitted in the area since then. It must be something else. Maybe a bird flew in through the air hole." They started to move off again.

Panic seized his mind. "No, they can't." Casca gave a low grunt, the kind a rooting hog might make. The sounds of movement stopped again.

One spoke to the other. "That was damned sure no bird. We'd better check it out."

The other hesitated. "I don't know. Ragnar said that cell wasn't to be opened."

His friend laughed. "What are you worried

about? There's nothing in there but the bones of a man long dead."

Footsteps again, nearer, then stopping. There was a grunt, as the man outside strained at the locked bar of the cell. It had been so long since it had been moved that the wood had swollen shut. Casca closed his eyes. *Please, open.* He heard a sliding sound, and the exhaling of the man's breath, straining to force the bar back. It took an eternity, longer than the years he had spent there, for the door to creakingly and laboriously swing open. One guard entered, his axe held low in front of him, although he wasn't really expecting any trouble. He was only being cautious and curious about the sounds that had come from inside the cell, which was supposedly unoccupied. Bony fingers wrapped around his throat, and thick fingernails dug in deep and squeezed until the cartilage crumpled. The man's fingers loosened their grip on his axe. The weapon fell with a dull thud onto the straw-matted floor, and still the squeezing continued until the world ended for the man in a burst of sparkling lights, then darkness. Casca let his first victim down and picked up the axe.

The dead man's companion called to him from where he was still holding the ropes of their prisoner near the next cell. "What is it? What did you find?"

A fearful apparition stepped out to answer his question. A terrifying, twisted, muscled skeleton of a man stepped forth, swinging an axe. The blade struck once at the collarbone and sunk midway into his chest, splitting him open. The last thing he felt was a foot on his chest as the blade was pulled out. Casca stood, the dripping axe in his hand. Covered with a crust of filth and dirt, his eyes wild, he raised the axe above his head and screamed. The new prisoner fainted.

Casca screamed again. The years of hate and frustration burst forth in a cry he couldn't stop . . . *"Lida!"*

In the Great Hall above, it was feast day—a day to celebrate the coming of the summer solstice under the auspices of a druid priest. For a moment, several of the guests stopped their drinking. What was it that they heard coming to them faintly above the clamor of the revelers? Probably nothing. But still, for that moment it left them chilled. Then they returned to the business at hand, drinking and feasting in honor of their host.

Ragnar sat at the center of the table. He had heard nothing. As was his pleasure, his daughter sat beside him to play hostess, with her sightless gaze resting upon nothing. For her, the world was as dead as her eyes, and she cared not what she did.

Another had heard the sound and felt not a shiver of fear, but one of anticipation. Glam stood near the corridor leading to the Hall. He moved to the guarded, bolted door in the feasting room that led to the dungeon below. As always, there were two armed men standing there. The door could only be opened from the outside. Several times he had tried to figure a way to get to the dungeon below, but there were always too many sentries on duty to insure any chance of success. And the men at the door weren't the only ones so employed; there were others below them. He had obeyed Casca's last words and waited, but now the waiting was about to end. The faint cry of Lida's name, reaching through the din of the feasting, told him Casca was coming and he must make ready to help him. Glam smiled a death's-head leer at old Ragnar's back and loosened the thongs holding his great axe to his side. *Soon, you swine. Casca is coming,* he thought. Glam moved closer to the guarded doorway, smiling at the guards, a horn of mead in his paw. He grinned knowingly. . . .

Chapter Nine

Glam chewed his mustache and watched Ragnar worrying at a beef bone like one of his dogs, and bellowing in raucous laughter at a story told him by one of his warrior captains. Glam took a pull from his horn and wiped the foam from his face with the back of one hairy hand. *Soon, you dirty bastard, soon. For two years, I have waited and done your dirty work and kissed your ass. But that is just about over now.* Muted groans from the other side of the door brought his and the two guards' heads around. The guards merely looked somewhat confused and bored, but Glam knew. Deep in his heart, he knew what was now on the other side of that massive oaken door—*death!*

The slide bar moved an inch back and forth but it couldn't be opened except from this side and Glam knew that now was the time. Moving closer to the guards, he laughed out loud. Bellowing laughter as if he had just seen or thought of something terribly funny. He roared with mirth and lurched toward the guards. They grinned and began to laugh a little, not knowing why they laughed, but the giant's obvious good humor was contagious. Glam leaned a heavy arm on the shoulder of the nearest man. "Jonash," he addressed the smiling guard, "you won't believe what's going to happen." The laughter rolled forth from him again. "You just won't believe it." He wiped a tear from his eye with his free hand, the other holding the mead, almost spilling over.

Jonash couldn't keep back a chuckle. "Why then, tell me, you great hairy old walrus. What wouldn't I believe?"

Glam almost fell over laughing. "Why, that you're going to die, you fool, and soon."

Confusion broke over the warrior's face; a touch of anger in his voice. He didn't like people making jokes at his expense. "And just how do you know that?"

Glam leaned heavier on his shoulder, his hand gripping hard. "Because, I'm going to kill you."

The latch bar on the door rattled again. The other guard merely looked bored. They all knew that Glam had a penchant for practical jokes and as long as he wasn't involved, he really didn't give a damn.

Jonash was getting pissed. "Knock off that crap, Glam. I don't like that kind of talk, even if you are joking."

Glam roared with glee. "But that's what's so funny, you little swine." He straightened up and threw the half-filled horn of mead into the man's face. "I'm not joking." Before either one could move, the great axe was free of its strap and swinging up to slice off the side of the blinded man's head. Then, with a quick turning of the wrist, the axe, without being brought back up or down, was heading into the open mouth of the other guard. The thick blade broke teeth and bone on its way to reach the spinal cord in the back of the man's neck.

Neither one made a sound in their dying. What little sound there had been of their falling was covered by the noise of the revelers.

Glam moved one of the bodies out of the way of the door and put his hand on the latch that would release what he knew was waiting on the other side. He whispered at the door, "Casca, it's me, Glam. I'm going to open up, so don't start swinging. There's a party going on, and the hall is filled." The latch slid and the door swung open to the inside.

Standing there, lit by the glow of the torch, was Casca. Glam almost dropped his axe. His master looked more like a nightmare caricature of a man than the clean-shaven Roman he had fought beside so many times. Caked filth hung from his chest and body in clots, his hair and beard were wild and tangled, and he held a dripping axe in each hand. But the eyes were the worst. Deep-sunken, the gray blue in them was gone. They were as dark as the river Styx in which the fires of hell were ready to be set free. Words came out of the cracked lips, a dry whisper from the years of not speaking. Hoarse, the voice spoke: "Glam, it's good you waited. We have work to do this night."

Glam couldn't speak. Never in his worst dreams had he ever seen anything that looked like his master did now. He nodded his head in agreement and stepped back to let him enter. As a pebble tossed into a pond spreads an expanding ring of ripples over the surface, silence spread through the hall, as first one reveler, then another, saw the weird and fearful apparition step forward, moving slowly, feet shuffling, as if the beast were terribly weary and running out of strength. The creature came closer to the center of the table. The increasing silence finally reached the ears of Ragnar. He stopped in his feeding. A piece of unchewed meat dropped from his open mouth to land on the table.

Casca stood in the center of the Hall. His eyes, running over the faces of the feasters, stopped on the face of Lida. She was more beautiful than he had remembered. Her head was turned, she seemed to be listening to the silence. A look of wonder played across her features. He moved to lock his gaze on that of Ragnar. Ragnar may have been a cruel brute, but he was no coward. The thing of skin and protruding ribs that stood before him had at first startled him. The bloody axes said that it was dangerous, but no more than many he had faced and killed. And from the look of the creature, it couldn't have much strength in it. Maybe it was some kind of joke.

One of Ragnar's mastiffs moved out from under the table where it had been feeding on scraps. A brindle-colored, thick-necked animal, it moved stiff-leggedly closer to the man in the center of the hall. Its nose tasted the strange odor, and its muzzle curled back in a snarl to show yellow canines. There was something about this man that was wrong.

Casca watched the approach of the fighting dog, his eyes on the animal. His lips, too, drew back in a snarl. A low growl came from inside, never rising to much more than a barely audible level, but enough for the dog to understand and fear.

The beast turned its eyes away from Casca. Its tail going down between its legs, it began to back away. It smelled no fear on this man, only the taste of death. The dog's growls slowly changed to the thin whimpers of fear that it hadn't made since it was a pup and had been faced down by one of the older dogs. It knew it was no match for this man. The dog's body assumed the position of submission, its spine curved and its tail between the legs. It slowly backed away, continuing to make the puppy noises. It would have no part of this. It left the hall to find a place to hide outside.

This more than the filthy starved caricature himself brought a sense of caution to Ragnar. There was a strange feeling to the silent man in this Hall. Something he had never experienced before. An aura that one might find while walking through a field of ancient battles where warriors lay dead with their weapons beneath one's feet.

Ragnar spoke, no trace of humor in his voice now. "And just what are you?" He turned his attention to his guests. "Have some of you thought to play a joke on me?"

The creature interrupted him. His voice was a dry husky whisper that everyone in the room could clearly hear. "What am I? I am the death that walks at every man's shoulder. I am the bearer of silence and the end to pain." He raised the axe in his right hand and pointed the spiked end at Ragnar. "I am Casca."

Lida's lips let free a small cry at the name, but was quickly silenced by Ragnar with a back hand across her mouth. He growled low and dangerously. "This is a poor joke, wretch. And I find it not to my liking. The Roman dog is long dead by my order."

Casca laughed, a thin bitter sound that sent chills up the backs of the less hearty there. "So you did order. But I live. . . . And now, it is your turn to die." He leaped forward, axes swinging. One would not have thought that he would have had enough strength in his thin knobby arms and wrists to lift even one of the heavy-bladed battle axes, but he did and more.

Two men died with their smashed heads laid open and their brains mingled with their dinner. Glam had moved behind the feasting table and was waiting for Casca's move. When it came he was ready.

Casca leaped upon the table, scattering bowls and flagons. Ragnar fell over on his back in his haste to get up, and the bony man was instantly on him. He had lost one axe when it stuck in the brain case of one of Ragnar's bodyguards. With the remaining one, he used the side and knocked Ragnar to his stomach, holding him there with the spiked point at the base of his neck. Glam had moved to cover him. The guests and their ladies did nothing. They knew that to move was to invite death.

Casca stood, sides heaving, over the object of his anger. "You would starve me and blind your own daughter." A beef bone, the size of a big man's forearm, fell from the table to rest beside Ragnar. There were still some chunks of meat on it. Even at this moment, the sight of the first food he had been near in two years was too much. Keeping the spike at the neck of Ragnar, he picked up the bone and began to gnaw on the large knuckled joint. The meat was half raw. If it hadn't been filled with red blood, there would have been no way he could have swallowed it with his dry throat. But the fat and blood aided its descent into his gut, where his stomach juices attacked the first real bite of food they had seen since his confinement. Ragnar squirmed under the point of the spike digging into the back of his neck, his beard and face pressed firmly into the straw covered floor. One of Ragnar's bodyguards, a man almost as big as

Glam with a face as red as his and a full, flame-colored beard and mustache, lunged over the table at Casca to free his master. Moving his axe from Ragnar's neck to face the attacker, Casca swung, bringing the blade down with such force that it split the man's head into two parts and buried itself four inches in the solid oak table.

Roaring, Ragnar jumped up from the floor and scrambled to his feet. Casca, without thinking, let go of the stuck axe and swung the beef bone; he wasn't going to let Ragnar get away. The knobbed knuckle of the bone struck Ragnar across the forehead, reeling him back. Casca switched hands, putting the bone into his right and grabbing Ragnar by his beard, then pulled him onto his knees and came down once more with the bone. This time, the knuckle hit with a crack that could be heard a hundred yards away. Ragnar's forehead split under the blow. He died instantly, faster than Casca would have killed had he had the choice, but no matter; the rotten old bastard was dead. He tossed the bone beside the body and worked the axe out of the table. No one else had moved. He turned to the stunned feasters.

"You women may leave, and take Lida with you."

Lida began to protest, wanting to know what was happening, but Casca silenced her.

"We will have time later. Obey me now. I still have some work to finish. Now go."

The women obeyed, glad to be out of the room. The door swung shut behind them. The men made no protest. They might have supported the cruel reign of Ragnar, but they were still men of the north and born to battle. They would stay though death would come in the next few minutes.

Casca uprighted Ragnar's overturned chair and sat down, watching the men he and Glam would soon fight. Stretching over, he took a flagon of mead and drank deeply, swallowing repeatedly, his eyes never leaving the faces of the men he would kill. He took a roast bird and stuffed it into his mouth, chewing some pieces and swallowing some of it whole. Even the bones he ground between his teeth. There were no sounds but those of breathing and his eating. Color was beginning to return to his face, strength flowing fresh to withered limbs. His mouth still hungered, but his shrunken stomach could hold no more. He wiped his fingers on the sleeve of the red-bearded man he had killed, to rid them of grease. He would need dry palms for this night's work.

Glam stood behind him, axe swinging slowly to and fro, waiting. He too had waited long for this night; a few minutes more or less made no difference.

Ragnar's men waited also until Casca had finished his meal. It seemed to take much longer than it actually did, but they were in no rush; eternity they knew was not far away.

Casca raised himself from the table, his eyes never leaving the waiting warriors. He spoke with renewed strength. "Well, gentlemen, shall we get on with it?"

One by one, the warriors rose and moved around to the front of the table. There had been eleven guests. Now eight stood in a rank waiting. They had drawn their weapons and stood ready.

One elder warrior, with more gray in his beard than the others, looked closely at the face of the man behind the table, and said, "Aye, it is you, though we were sure you died long ago." A smile played at his mouth. "Indeed, you look more like a corpse than old Ragnar does. He, no doubt, did you and the lady a great wrong, and we did nothing to stop him. He was our sworn liege, no matter what he did, and ours was a blood oath. Now, it is up to you. I know that there is something within you that we cannot win against, some force that sustains you when others would die. It has been said the gods have touched you. Perhaps that is so. At any rate, I know that what happens now is in your hands. Whether we live or die is your decision. I know we may not be leaving this room alive, but you will know that you have had a fight against men."

The old warrior raised his sword in salute and threw his cloak back out of the way of his sword arm. Then he bowed and stepped forward. "Let me be the first. As the eldest here, I claim that right. . . ."

Casca moved around the table, Glam close to his side. "Old man, you have proclaimed your guilt through your own lips. *Blood oath.*" The words dripped with contempt from the Roman's mouth. "There is no oath so binding that it justifies pain only for another's pleasure. It was your support that permitted the beast to live. You could have stopped him, but it was easier to go along with him, to do nothing, in the name of an oath. Well, hear mine.

"I swear, before all the gods and demons of the world, that not one of you will leave this room alive. That here and now, you will pay your bill. This night, you have been judged, and the sentence is *death.*"

Outside the Hall door, guards had gathered,

ready to attack. They had heard from the women
of Ragnar's death at the hand of the Roman. They
made no attempt to enter. With Ragnar's death,
they owed him nothing. His daughter was now mistress of this house and, on her command, they
stood silent, with the others, waiting.

Then came the sounds of battle, swords against
axes, cries to the gods and Wotan to give them
strength, and, inevitably, the sound of men dying.
At first, there were the sounds of single combat
only. Then came the cries of multiple voices joined
in battle. Then silence, terrible silence that meant it
was all over. Still, they waited until the door was
opened by Glam, who was torn and cut in a dozen
places, his arms and chest covered not only with his
own blood, but with that of the men lying in broken profusion inside the Hall. His dripping axe left
a trail of thick red spots behind him.

Casca was sitting at the head of the table, one of
the dead men's cloaks about him, head between his
hands, weary. It was over. The old warrior had
been right about one thing. The corpses on the
floor were men. At least, they had been. It was
done with.

Glam spoke to Lida. "It is over. Go to your
rooms. Now is not the time to talk to him, when he
still has the smell of death on him. He would not
wish it so. Go, and on the morrow all will be made
right." He swelled himself to his full height and
spoke to all gathered. "Casca, the Walker, is now
lord of Helsfjord and master of all that was
Ragnar's. He claims this by right of the sword. If
any would dispute his claim, let him come forth
with sword in hand or leave. Any who remain will
serve him, as I do.

"What say you?" The waiting guards raised their spears and axes in salute. "We serve. Casca is lord of the Hold. . . ."

The Field of Runes was named for the stones carved with the angular strokes and squiggles of the northern folk writings. Only a few could translate their meanings, some of which reached far back into antiquity and were said to be the records of the deeds of great heroes and kings.

Of all present, only Hagdrall could read them with any degree of proficiency. Most had been written when the druids were highly respected throughout the northlands and even into Gaul. Now they were being driven back into a few strongholds. Here, in Scandia, and in Britain, they had their last refuge from the edicts of Rome and were determined to hang on to what remained of their influence as they competed with the other gods for the mind of the people.

Once they had controlled the destinies of kings. Now, in most places, they were little more than figureheads, and, like all priests of dying religions that were losing followers, they didn't like it a damned bit.

Hagdrall had spent years establishing his influence over Ragnar and his people, and felt no desire to return to the lesser position of just being around to bless weddings or say the funeral rites over the dead, though he wouldn't have minded doing those rites over Casca. Nothing had been right since the Roman had screwed up their plans to marry Lida off to Icenius—a vantage point from which the druids might have been able to begin to reestablish themselves in their former position of respect and power. Now, there were only a few each year that came to be initiated into the rites and to perform the mysteries.

He hadn't even been asked to perform the wedding ceremony for Casca and Lida. Hagdrall grumbled to himself beneath his beard, "That's all right, Roman, I've not finished with you yet." The wedding proceedings were nearing their conclusion.

The ceremony binding Casca the Roman and Lida of the sightless eyes had come down from the beginnings of the Norse past. At one time when those of the nobility were to wed, there had been much blood shed in sacrifices. In time, due to the unwillingness of the villagers to participate in these activities just to insure the goodwill of the gods and spirits, the practice was discontinued and animals took the place of humans. The ceremony remained about the same. Priests would chant and plead with the spirits, doing the secret things that made them priests, then the animals would be disembowled and the entrails inspected for omens. Naturally the signs were always favorable, as bad news would have reduced the amount of the gifting the priests would have received from the couples' families and friends.

Casca had nothing against the sacrificing of goats and cattle, as the flesh would be consumed by the wedding guests and not the flames of the sacrificial fires. For the rest, he had seen the same ceremony with minor variations among many peoples during his travels. The villagers didn't mind too much when he said he would use a village elder rather than bring in another druid for the rites.

This last night before his wedding looked like it was going to be a long one. Glam would hear of nothing else. He and the men of the hold would drink and feast until it came time for Casca to enter into the bonds of domestic servitude. Glam, as usual, had nothing good to say about anything concerning weddings. But Casca knew it was all show and that Glam would have happily beat the brains out of anyone who even hinted they would disrupt the ceremony. The old heathen was as happy as a child behind his gruff manner and well pleased to see Casca acquire that which he wanted most in the world, Lida.

A double row of maidens, dressed alike in flowing white robes and fall flowers in their hair, sang songs of love and devotion. A white ram was sacrificed and the senior elder of the largest village was asked to read the signs while its innards were dragged out into the open air.

"That should have been my job. That ignorant dirt farmer can't possibly know the first thing about divining." Hagdrall drew to the rear of the proceedings.

Under the elder's watchful gaze, the couple exchanged salt, earth, and fire—a simple ceremony, and then it was done. They were now one. According to the rites of Mother Earth, they were joined until Father Death separated them.

Casca took his bride into his arms and gently kissed each of her sightless eyes, then her mouth, marveling at the sweetness of her breath.

Glam sniffled in his beard. Being the sentimental slob that he was, he always cried at weddings.

Chapter Ten

It was not too long after Casca believed he had finally settled into the comfortable mold of married life, when he and Glam embarked on a hunting trip to get away from the mounting duties of the hold. Even Lida had insisted that Casca take off a few days and get rid of some of the tension that was building up in him from having to deal with the everyday problems of running even a domain as small as his. She knew that it wasn't the line of work he was cut out for, but he did do his best to be fair and just.

There was some reluctance on his part to leave Lida behind, but she assured him that she would be well taken care of and that it made good sense for him to get familiar with the terrain around Helsfjord in the event of trouble. Casca couldn't deny that. A good soldier always checked out the lay of the land—though in Glam's interpretation that meant the hottest-blooded woman he could find.

They set off shortly after sunrise, packs slung over their shoulders, swords at their hips, and boar spears held close at hand. It felt good. From the first step out of the gray confines of the hold, Casca could feel the weight of his responsibilities drop off him. As for Glam, Casca wasn't sure the man-beast knew how to worry. Each step out into the woods was lighter than the one preceding it.

Glam thumped his barrel chest and breathed deeply. "Ahhhhh! That's better than the smell of wood smoke and baby piss in the nostrils all day, is it not?"

Casca had to agree.

The day sparkled with a clear crystal sky above them, and the last of the ground fog of the morning rose to be whisked away at the tops of the pines and oaks. Forest sounds gently greeted them as they made their way with no real direction in the mind. The singing of birds and the quick rustling of small animals scurrying away at their approach were welcome sounds to their ears.

They trekked all that day, stopping only once for a short breather. Crossing the ridges and valleys, Casca enjoyed the feel of the strain, the aching of unused muscles. He hadn't had much exercise since the time he had been put in the dungeon, and had had damned little after taking over control of Helsfjord except for the delightful exercises Lida put him through. For a woman so fragile in appearance, to his delight she had an amazing amount of strength and endurance. More than once she had forced the tough, lumpy-muscled exgladiator to the thumbs gesture asking for mercy, which she seldom granted.

A couple of hours before dark they settled on a sheltered glen to make camp. It had a small, clear, cold stream, which fed into a larger one that eventually led to the sea.

Glam left Casca to set up camp and headed downstream a ways to see what he could scrounge up for chow. He looked in the shallow waters of the stream until he found what he was looking for. Giving a yell for Casca, the Roman joined him and looked to where Glam's dirty-nailed finger was pointing in the water. Several good-sized trout were lying just under the surface, almost motionless. They moved only enough to keep their position in the running stream. Glam told Casca to keep an eye on the fish while he went a little further downstream. Casca didn't know what Glam had in mind, but there was usually a reason for everything Glam did, even if it did sometimes take years to figure out just what it was.

Glam stopped about fifty feet down and rapidly built a small barricade of stones across the stream. When he had finished, he yelled for Casca to chase the fish down to him.

Casca jumped into the chilled waters, which reached just above his ankles, and started the startled trout down to his bearish companion. With a quick flick of their tails the fish were gone, streaking through the shallows. Casca followed, splashing with his feet and cursing the chill. He arrived in time to see Glam bent over, his arms groping in the stream. First one, then another of the silver bodies were knocked out of the water by Glam's paws. When the fish reached his small dam, they could go no further and were trapped between Glam and Casca. Casca was sure that Glam had bear blood in him as the barbarian bent over the water, arms swinging as Casca had seen bears do when fishing. They would make a swipe with their paws and send a fish flying onto the shore. Casca left the wet fishing to Glam, who was doing just fine in his groping. He contented himself with

keeping the fish from getting past him back up-
stream, though several did manage to flick their
way between his legs and escape. In no time at all
Glam had enough fat trout lying on the grass to
make a large enough meal to satisfy even his
oversized appetite.

That night they fed well on baked trout. Glam
had packed the bodies in mud and then put them in
the coals of their campfire to cook. Casca cursed
between clenched teeth as he burned his fingers in
his impatience to get at the succulent white meat
beneath the baked mud shell. When he finally got
the shells opened, the smell of the fish mingled with
the clean odor of the pines, and his mouth was watering in anticipation. They spiced the fish with a
touch of rock salt and for once, even Glam seemed
content with the quality of the food. It had been a
good day and they were tired, but it was the kind of
tiredness that felt good. With full stomachs, they
slept under the open night sky, enjoying the quiet
of the evening, which was broken only by the
crackling of the embers in their campfire.

Noon of the following day found them high on a
ridge looking out over a primeval forest far below
in a valley broken with glades and streams. The
wind was cool, giving them a clean, fresh feeling as
it brushed over their faces. It was a time to be
savored. After the violence and bloodshed of the
past months, moments like these were too few not
to be treasured.

With some degree of reluctance they headed
back down into the shadows of the trees on the
other side of the mountain. Glam whistled off-key
between his furry lips, trying to imitate the trillings
of the birds with no success, though he thought he

performed the act to perfection.

For three days they wandered with no plan, seeing no sign of humans other than the distant smoke of an occasional village, which they avoided. Casca wanted no contact with people. Where men were to be found, so was trouble, and he had no desire to involve himself in anything that would spoil their journey.

At the base of the ridge the deer trail they had been following narrowed, leaving only a small space on which the ledge they were on could be crossed. There their peace and tranquility was broken by the sounds of men coming from the other direction. Casca was about to make the decision to go back the way they had come and leave the deer trail for the quiet of the woods, but it was too late; he had been spotted. A furred, spear-toting warrior that could have been a smaller version of Glam broke into view.

Casca and Glam stopped, as did the warrior, who was facing them from about thirty feet. Rapidly the lone warrior was joined by others until five armed men faced them.

Glam mumbled to Casca to watch out. These were Saxons and they were too far from their own lands to be nothing more than tourists. And they were still inside the boundaries of Helsfjord. The five scowled at them from under shaggy brows. They talked in whispers among themselves when there came another movement behind them and several women and children came into view with another Saxon behind them. Glam spoke softly. "They're slavers. Perhaps the smoke we saw yesterday wasn't from campfires,"

Casca agreed. If the captives were from one of

his villages he would have to do something about it. It was his duty. He called out to the Saxons, "Peace, warriors, and welcome to my lands."

The Saxons talked among themselves a moment, and then one stepped out to the forefront. He was a few inches taller than the others although still shorter than Glam, but he made up for what he lacked in height with the width of his body. Even under his fur robes, thick bands of muscle were easily visible, especially those that led from his neck down to his massive, thick, sloping shoulders. As with all his companions, he had a full growth of reddish-blond beard with a fierce sweeping mustache. He responded to Casca's welcome. "And whose land is that?"

Casca shifted his boar spear to his right hand.

The motion did not go unnoticed by the slavers. They too loosened the thongs holding their axes and shifted their spears to a handier position.

"It is mine, Casca of Helsfjord."

The Saxon called back, "You lie. Helsfjord is ruled by Ragnar."

Glam chose that time to speak up. "It was ruled by Ragnar and Ragnar was killed by this man, who has claimed all that was Ragnar's and has taken Ragnar's own daughter to wed."

Casca cut Glam's oration short with a wave of his hand. He eyed the Saxons opposite him. "Where did you obtain your captives?"

The Saxons preferred not to have any trouble if they could avoid it, and their leader said, "Some day's journey from here where we paid good silver for them."

A woman in the back cried out a name before the rope around her neck choked off any further response. But it was enough. The name she spoke was *Lida*. Upon closer inspection, Casca discovered that this slave was indeed one of the Lady Lida's personal handmaids.

Glam moved to present a smaller target by turning his body slightly to the side.

Casca called back, his voice friendly. "Why, then, we have no quarrel if you bought and paid for your slaves like honest men. Travel on, Saxons." Casca turned from them only to lower his body down. In the next instant he whipped back around, hurling the boar spear underhanded. Before the Saxon leader had a chance to react the spear had implanted itself in his chest. He wondered briefly about the pain in his back. He died not knowing that the head of the spear had torn clear through him and was sticking out a foot from his spine.

Glam bellowed and hurled his own spear, which entered a warrior's stomach and kept on going until at least half of its own length penetrated out the Saxon's back. He always had to try and outdo Casca. Grinning, he spoke to his friend. "Two down and four to go, so don't you get greedy now. Remember to save a little for me."

Glam rushed to the front and blocked the trail with his body, his axe already swinging with irresistible force, smashing down the guard of the two Saxons facing him. One had barely managed to swing his buckler off his shoulder when his face disappeared in a bloody whirl. The other suffered a quicker death than his gurgling comrade when Glam split him from pate to chin.

Reluctantly he had to let Casca in on the fight when he stopped for a moment to work the axe out of the skull by stepping on the Saxon's face to hold him still while twisting the thick blade free from the bone.

Of the remaining Saxons, one came on with a half-hearted sweep of his long sword, but Casca could see in the man's eyes that he was already dead in his mind. So to save the poor soul from any further confusion, Casca dispatched him with little effort, blocking the long sword. Then with a single long step inside the man's guard he thrust his own short sword up at an angle where it could reach the doomed warrior's heart with little trouble. The man coughed up a spurt of blood and died without further ado.

The single surviving Saxon gave up completely and released the rope holding his string of captives together. He chose the better part of valor by leaving his weapons behind and disappeared back down the way he had come as fast as his hairy legs would take him. Glam wanted to go after him now that he had his axe clear of the bony mess it had been stuck in, but Casca stopped him with the comment that the survivor's story might deter others from coming to Helsfjord on slave raids.

After releasing the captives to return to their villages, he and Glam continued on their interrupted journey. Glam was in high spirits after the day's bloody work. Casca was a little less so but he did have to admit that a good fight did wake up the blood.

The trouble behind them, they wandered on for two more days until they were near the boundaries of the Helvetii. From there they would go no further. It was time to return to Helsfjord with the regret that always comes when one has to give up the free life and return to the pressures of normal life. They were just about ready to turn back and head for home when Glam told him to stop. He had heard horses and voices from across a small glade. Glam crept up a little closer and called Casca to him.

The noises came from a band of traders bringing goods from Gaul to trade for whatever they could find of value in Germania. Gold, silver, and amber were the most sought-after, but they would take amounts of rare furs back with them and nearly anything else the tribesmen might have acquired on their occasional forays across the Rhine or Danube. Glam asked Casca if it was all right to see if the merchants had any wine in their packs.

Casca agreed; they looked to be legitimate traders. True, they did have a couple of tough-looking Marcomanni with them as bodyguards and guides, but that was only natural.

He and Glam made their way to the encampment walking through knee-high grass damp with dew. They called out their coming to avoid being speared by an overanxious guard. They stopped while still out of spear range and called out once more, requesting permission to enter the camp.

Permission was granted, and Casca, followed by the hulking Glam, entered the camp. They were greeted by wary but not necessarily hostile looks. After all, there were only two of them and the camp guards could surely handle them if the need arose.

The merchant whose expedition it was came forth to greet them. "Ave, brave warriors. I am Lucius Decius, an honest merchant of the world come to exchange my wares for the goods the people of these parts may wish to part with. I'll take almost anything—gold, silver, slaves, amber, or what have you. Now, what have you need of, my friends? Thread, needles, or cloth for your women-folk? Or perhaps fine blanks of Roman steel from which your smiths can fashion blades to your own taste?''

The balding stocky merchant went on with his spiel. Casca could tell the man was a confirmed horsetrader. He asked to see some of the bolts of cloth. Perhaps there would be something worth taking back to Lida. Glam asked if there was by chance any wine in the casks and kegs he could see lying about the camp.

Decius replied that certainly he had brought with him, at great personal expense, a few kegs of good wine which, as he was sure the noble German knew, helped to make a day's trading go easier. And for a man such as he, Decius had even stashed away a few flagons of an especially fine and rare Lesbos.

Glam rattled his purse, which gave off the clear tinkling sound of silver coins, and gently requested that he might be permitted a sip of the good stuff before buying. The tinkling of hard cash brought an immediate affirmative response from Decius, who quickly regretted his action, as Glam's sip could take in more than most grown men could in two full swallows. Decius grimaced at every bob of the German's Adams apple as first one skin then another went flacid. It was only after a bout of hard haggling that Decius was able to just break even on selling Glam two small kegs of his cheapest wine.

Casca was ready by then with his choice of material. They settled down to dealing over the price of some of the blue damask interwoven with threads of silver, which Casca thought would go well with Lida's fair hair and complexion. Casca made his offer on the cloth and Decius agreed. They spit in their palms, slapped hands, and the deal was closed.

Casca had just packed the cloth away in his kit when he heard a voice just out of sight in one of the merchant's tents. A man's voice was pleading in Latin. Casca walked over to the tent before he could be stopped and threw open the flap. A small balding man with only a fringe of gray hair surrounding his pate was on his knees trying to clean up a mess where he had spilled a bowl of stew. One of the merchant's hirelings was laying it on with a staff across the man's shoulders and cursing with every thump of the club. His efforts were halted by Casca's hand grasping his wrist and squeezing, though not too hard; he didn't want to break the bones. The hireling grunted in pain and tried to break out of the crushing grip, but the years Casca had spent at the oars of the Imperial war galleys of Rome had given him a grip that few could equal. As the bodyguard was forced to let go of his club, he dropped squealing to his knees alongside of the man he had been beating.

Others of the camp came rushing to the tent at the sound of the disturbance. Decius reached the tent first, and spoke. "Why have you interfered with the chastising of my property?"

Casca looked at the little bald man still trying to clean up the mess on the tent floor. There was intelligence in the sad brown eyes and it had been a long time since he had spoken the tongue of Rome.

He turned to the merchant, still keeping a grip on the moaning guard's wrist in one hand while his other touched the hilt of his sword. Glam had moved to the rear of Decius' group, holding his boar spear in his left hand while raising his axe to his shoulder with the other.

Casca spoke to Decius. "This man is your property?"

Decius replied that he was in fact his property and had a proper bill of sale to prove it. Decius noted Casca's interest in the slave and his merchant's mind went to work. "Yes, he is my slave and an extremely valuable one that would bring an excellent price, as he knows both numbers and writing in Latin and in Greek. A man such as this is worth more than rubies on this side of the Rhine."

Casca spoke to the slave in Latin, keeping an eye on Decius and his men. "What's your name, man?"

The slave straightened himself up as much as he could, rubbing his sore shoulders. "I am Corio the builder."

"What kind of builder?"

Corio sensed that he might have a chance of exchanging masters, and from the way this barbarian had stopped his being beaten, it might be a change for the better. And the barbarian spoke Latin perfectly. "I can build many things, noble sir—fortifications and canals, though my best work has been in the shipyards of Ostia, where many of my ships have sailed safely on the seas thanks to my good works."

Casca thought it over for a moment. A shipbuilder is he? He turned his attention back to the merchant. "How much for the fellow? I may have need for such as he."

Decius hesitated. These two savages were poorly dressed, but appearances could be deceiving, and they had paid for what they had bought in good silver. "I would have three gold ounces for him, and he is a bargain at that price, for I have had to feed and care for him the last two months."

Casca reached into the bottom of his purse and withdrew his only two gold ounces and tossed them to the merchant, who deftly snatched them out of the air.

"I'll give you two and make you the offer that if you come to Helsfjord, you will be well received, for I am master there."

One of the guards whispered in Decius' ear when he heard the name of Helsfjord. "I think it would be wise to accept his offer. If this man's name is Casca, he is not to be toyed with. I have heard of how he came to power there and it was over the bodies of those who opposed him. It is also said he has a giant as a companion who is nearly as dangerous as he is. The builder is not worth any of our lives. Even if we won, the price would be great."

Decius pursed his lips. "And what is your name, noble sir?"

The blue-gray eyes turned cold. He knew they were weighing the odds. "I am Casca of Helsfjord and this is my sword companion, Glam, son of Halfdan the Ganger. Do we have a deal, merchant, or do we make a trade that would be hard on everyone?"

Decius swallowed a taste of bitter bile; he was a trader, not a warrior. The sight of blood, especially his own, gave him fits of nausea.

Casca loosened his sword in its scabbard a bit more.

Decius hastily responded, "Of course, of course. You may have the man for two gold ounces and welcome, Lord Casca. By all means, he is yours." Decius entered his tent and returned after a moment handing over to Casca the papers of ownership.

Casca told his new slave to get his things together. They would be leaving now. Corio scurried to do his new master's bidding. It didn't take long, as he only had the plain rough-woven tunic on his back, a threadbare cloak, and a few scrolls of numbers that he would need in following his craft.

Casca led the way out of the camp with Corio in the center and Glam bringing up drag, still keeping a wary eye on those in the camp. The merchant sighed a breath of relief that things hadn't turned out much worse. He had even made a small profit on the slave. He turned to his subordinates with the orders to break camp. He looked back longingly to the south where the civilized lands lay. It was always chancy when you dealt with savages, but that was the way of things. If you could survive a trip or two into the dark forests of Germania, a man could make enough profit to set up a proper trading house. From there he would be able to take his ease and send others out to do the hard and dangerous work of bartering with the savages. He was especially glad that he brought with him a couple of packs of mirrors, for each of those would bring almost as much as did the slave.

On their return to the hold of Helsfjord Casca had many hours in which to learn of how Corio had come to his unhappy condition. The little man was a habitual gambler, a disease that afflicted many Romans. The only ones Casca had ever met that were worse than the Romans were the Arabs. Corio had been legally sold to settle the debts owed his creditors. An official ruling from the magistrate at Ostia had been forwarded to the shipyards of Messilia where Corio had been on a subcontracting job laying the keels for a couple of fat merchantmen. Without any fuss he had been duly informed of his changed status and sold the next day to the trader Decius, who was even then on his way to the frontier.

Corio's pudgy face flushed from the strain of using so many muscles he never knew he had, climbing up one crest only to go down and find another awaiting him even more rugged than the previous one. But there was one bright spot when Casca told him he could have his freedom after three years, or sooner if he could save enough to pay him back the money spent on his purchase. All in all, Corio felt he had been lucky in having the Roman barbarian purchase him—not that he had had any choice in the matter. So there was no sense of being lost when he finally saw the gray stone walls of Helsfjord. Quickly he had learned that his new master and his friendly giant weren't going to hurt him. In fact, he felt less like a slave and more like one being invited to visit old friends, and he was anxious to meet the Lady Lida.

Chapter 11

Besides the great expanse across the Rhine known as Germania, there were also the lands bordering the Danube, that sister river of the Rhine, which ran thirteen hundred miles until it reached the Euxine Sea. Along its banks were found the savage lands of Thetia, Pannonia, Dalmatia, Dacia, Maesia, Thrace, and Macedon. Some of these lands had inhabitants that still savored the taste of human flesh. Others were remnants of ancient cultures far older than Rome that still influenced their lifestyles, such as Macedonia from which the noble Alexander derived his heritage.

The empire had brought much to the world, and even now was contributing greatly to the project of providing a modicum of civilization to those within its borders. The barbarians across the frontiers looked with envy upon the acquisitions of those that had placed their allegiance with the Eagles and had sworn fealty to the emperor of the world. While the barbarians hungered for their wealth, they also despised them for surrendering their pride and letting the Romans rule over them. Wealth flowed in a never-ending stream into the ports and cities of the empire.

Furs from Scythia, carpets from distant Babylon, the wealth of a thousand subject peoples filled the coffers of the imperial city of the Caesars. Trade goods came even from lands so distant that most thought them only to be myths.

Every year on the summer solstice, a fleet of ships would set their sails from Myos-hormos in Egypt to follow the winds that would carry them to the far island of Malabar, where they would trade for the wealth of the Orient. They brought back jade, precious stones, rare animals for the arena, and most valuable of all, silk. A pound of the fine material was equal in value to a pound of gold. In December or January, the ships would set sail again to let the changing currents of the winds return them home, from whence their previous cargo would eventually find its way to the bazaars and markets of Rome itself.

Trade was the life blood of the empire. Without it, the boundaries of the empire would soon have shrunk until it contained no more than the Seven Hills of Rome itself. One may take a land by conquest, but it cannot be held long without trade. Rome had not started out to be master of the world. She had only wanted to provide herself with secure borders. But she found that every time she conquered a savage or hostile land and absorbed it into the framework of her own empire, there was always another savage or hostile land lying just beyond. In order to secure the peace of the lands she had just acquired, she would have to fight and conquer those on the new frontiers.

In comparison, Casca's small lands were poor, but he was satisfied and indeed would have preferred not to have even the responsibility he did. The dreams of conquest and dynasty were not his. He knew he was not the stuff kings are made of. In his heart and mind, he was still a common soldier and was content with the things a soldier found pleasurable—a little wine from time to time, a roll in the hay with a willing wench, and a little time to occasionally lie in the sun and sleep. The business of ruling a small tribe was almost more than he could deal with. So he ruled as a simple soldier with few rules other than common sense. He was smart enough to know that what the Romans thought of as the good life would destroy his people. Strange, but he did think of them as his people. They were just simple folk with rough rules of honor and justice. They would not have the immunities to corruption that one would inherit if he was brought up in the cities of the empire. It was best for him to keep as much distance between them as he could from the civilizing influences of Rome. The rot would come soon enough without him helping it any. He had had no desire to affect the mantle of greatness, but fate always forced him into a path he would have preferred to avoid. He was content to be himself and no more.

But in Rome, the new emperor had a maggot that ate at his soul. Casca knew he came from common clay. The Emperor Maximim wore a heavy crown. Corio, the shipbuilder, had brought Casca up to date as best he could on what had transpired in the empire since he had crossed the Rhine those long years ago, and the news was not good.

Rome was decaying from the inside even faster than he had thought she would. He had first seen the rot setting in when he had served under the

Eagles of Avidius Cassius in Persia. In the last thirty years, there had been twelve emperors in Rome, and most had lasted no more than a year or two and some only a matter of days or weeks.

Currently the new master of the world was one Maximim. Born of the barbarian races, he now ruled over the noble bloodlines of the senate by virtue of his favor with the army, who had put him on the throne after watching the empire being sold to the highest bidder by the praetorian guards. They'd decided that Rome would be best served by one of their own—a soldier who had risen from the ranks and had proven his courage in battle fighting shoulder to shoulder along with them. The fact that he was not of fine and noble blood they considered to be in his favor. Maximim's mother was of the tribes of the Alani and his father was a Goth. During the reigns of Septimus and his son Severus, he had attained the high rank of centurion, but the raw sore of frustrated ambition always lay in the back of his thoughts. He'd waited patiently, building his reputation with the legions. Eating their food, and living in the same tents that sheltered the most common of his soldiers, he'd built a bond between him and the legion that he knew would one day serve him well. He waited, biding his time as emperors were assassinated or replaced, knowing the legions were growing ever more discontent with the weak selections of the senate and praetorians.

When Severus had returned from the Persian wars to conduct a new campaign against the German tribes, he had met with Maximim, then Commander of the Ninth Legion, on the banks of the Rhine.

There, when the troops were passing in review,

the legion spontaneously, or so it seemed, proclaimed Maximim emperor and proved their devotion to him by murdering Alexander Severus. Maximim was emperor, but the knowledge of his common blood ate at him and he soon set about eliminating anyone who could remind him of his less than noble lineage. While affecting the manners of the nobility in public, he still had the rough courage and temperament of his barbarian mother and father, and proved it time and again, not hesitating to proscribe on any pretext any who got in his way. He knew his power rested on the spears of the legions, and so he set about securing their loyalties even more by giving them donatives of money that they hadn't earned by service in battle. But Maximim forgot that when one gives money to a man who hasn't earned it, the man will take it, but will also grow to despise the giver as well as himself; and it's easier to get rid of the giver than eliminate oneself. It's also a lot less painful.

Maximim's biggest screw-up was when he set to melting down the statues of past emperors. That he might have gotten away with. But when he took to melting down the statues of the holy gods of Olympus and Rome itself, he went too far. When you get the priests after your ass, you don't last long in this world. He could order a man's wife and children sold into slavery to settle a debt. That wasn't too bad; the man would just usually grumble and bitch about it for a while. But when you messed with his gods, you'd find your ass in a sling soon enough, with the priests whipping it rather soundly. There have been few in history who ever survived the wrath of a righteous priest who has had his easy living taken away.

Casca shook his head and poured another mug of mulled wine spiced with a few bits of rare cloves for himself and Corio. Casca sipped, swallowed, and wondered. Why do men seek that which will destroy them? What is the drive that forces man to seek power over the bodies of even his friends and family, when they should know from history that the same power that they will hold so fleetingly will lead not only to their destruction, but to that of their own children and comrades. It would be better to have a small holding where one could watch his children, as well as his fields and herds, grow tall and strong in the sun, instead of having to worry about seeing them cut down before his eyes by those seeking to replace him on some decaying seat of senseless power.

Corio agreed with Casca's sentiments exactly. Bidding him good night, he stumbled off to his chambers to sleep off what he knew would be a bad head in the morning.

Chapter Twelve

Casca set about reforming the small group of warriors that served him. He kept forty warriors on full-time duty for the security of the hold and the valley.

They also served as a backup force for any of the villages that might come under attack. There were four villages in his valley and about two thousand people that paid him fealty. Out of that two thousand, he could field four hundred warriors if the need arose. That included males from sixteen to fifty. Casca restored the villagers the right of enforcing their own civil laws by the ancient tradition of a council of elders. He reserved the right of appeal for himself and was the only one able to pass down a judgment of death.

The villages were run under the tradition of village ownership of the tillable land. Each year, the elders would meet and decide how much each family needed for its purposes. The houses were mostly of stone and thatch. Many of them were half under the ground, this serving to keep out the worst of the winter chill. They were a tough people with rough rules of honor and chivalry. Of slaves, there were few. Casca himself only owned a half dozen.

His best acquisition was Corio, the Roman ship-builder, who helped redesign the shallow draft fishing boats and make them better able to deal with the wild currents and storms of the northern waters.

The older warriors were hard to train in new methods. Too long they had fought in the manner of their fathers. Like most of the barbarian tribes, they had little or no armor and went into battle protected at best with shields of wicker or wood with metal rims. Most of their swords were poor things of iron. Casca had more than once, in battle on the Rhine, seen a barbarian have to stop and try to straighten out his blade by placing his foot on it and bending it. The only blades of any worth were sold by traders and were jealously guarded by their fortunate owners. There were still quite a few of the old bronze swords with leaf-style blades around. But Corio also had a knowledge of metal-working, and soon had a small foundry started to produce better blades for Casca's warriors. He just about gave up on trying to discipline the elder warriors and concentrated most of his efforts on their children. It was easier to take a young mind and mold it. Selecting boys of ten to twelve, he made it an honor to be accepted into training. They were to be his insurance for the survival of Lida's people.

They had their fair share of enemies, and after Ragnar's death, several of his old enemies decided to try their luck, much to their regret. Though Casca couldn't get his warriors to obey the discipline of the legion, they still followed his orders better than they had anyone else's, and tried to do as he wished. It was just when the berserker rage came over them that they lost all control. He had managed to keep his young men out of the occasional call to arms for war against the Romans, knowing full well they would have little chance against the legions, even if they weren't as good as those he had served with so many years ago. The legions were still too well-trained for these raw warriors to be able to deal with with any hope of success. Besides, he still felt a sense of loyalty to the Eagles, even if they had treated him badly on more than one occasion. In his mind he was still a Roman soldier. No, he could best serve them by keeping them out of the wars, which came almost every spring.

Shields and spears on their shoulders, he marched his men out of the stone walls of the hold to the site where he had taken Lida as his bride. It took two hours to reach the clearing. This was a holy spot. Not so long ago, when the druids still practiced human sacrifice, it was here that each spring, before the first wild flowers appeared or the ground was broken for planting, a virgin would be sacrificed to Mother Earth. Indeed, the grass did seem to be a little richer and the leaves of the brush waxier in this spot. Now, the druids were no more than soothsayers and teachers. Before long they wouldn't even be that.

Casca walked over the ground they would soon be fighting on, looking at the way the Saxons must come, analyzing what he knew of their method of fighting. The Saxons had little use for archers; they preferred the sword, spear, and axe. They would form in a rough line at their end of the field and then start working themselves up to a killer pitch. Then they would start their advance, slowly at first, gaining speed until they charged, trying to overrun the defenders in a rush. Casca knew they would not rush until they were fairly close. He also knew they were pretty damned good with the throwing spear, and especially with the axe. They usually carried at least three or more axes. They would throw these in a wave, then rush. That would be the moment for him to win or lose.

Helsfjord was far enough away from Gaul so that there was little chance of any Roman army ever approaching them. His biggest worry was some of his neighbors, in particular, the Saxon tribes to the north of him. Every spring they made more advances. If they'd had a strong central leader, Casca was sure they would have been able to take over almost all of Germania. But lucky enough, they, as with the rest of the tribes, were factionalized into small tribal groupings—often no more than individual households that would come together only for a short time in order to make raids and then would return to their homes with their booties or their dead to wait till the next time.

His first real confrontation was with his Saxon neighbors along the coast. He had twice sent their emissaries back with his rejection of their offer for an alliance to raid other tribes. Casca desired no more land. The more you had, the greater your problems. Mostly, he wanted to have a time of peace to be able to stay with Lida. But each season, this was denied him as he had to take to the field to protect his small domain. The Saxons had called him a usurper who had no right to the hold, and were determined to rid their lands of him and all who supported the foreigner.

The Saxons were on the march. He had known for some time that matters must come to a head, and had done the best he could to prepare for it. By now, most of the ten- and twelve-year-olds were grown enough to fill his ranks. True, he had only about fifty of them, but they would be his mainstay, the rock upon which the rest of his small army would depend if they were to have any hope of victory against the larger forces that were even now only two days march from his borders. The youngsters were eager as only young men can be for the coming battle. As in the legion, he formed them into units of ten. For the last seven years, he had drilled them endlessly in attack and defense. Corio had made for them his finest weapons and shields. The swords were longer than his own Gladius and the shields were smaller than the Roman models. He had found a preference for the smaller round buckler. The large shields were of more use when you had greater numbers and were fighting from a predominantly defensive posture. He didn't have enough manpower for that luxury. He would have to rely on a more mobile approach to warfare than that.

His scouts reported that the Saxons would be coming from the long end of the valley through the field of Runes.

He decided that was where the battle would take place. That morning, his small force moved to take up positions. To guard the hold, he left behind the older, more headstrong warriors with orders that if they lost the fight, they were to take Lida away and sail to Britannia.

He had fielded 175 of his men, taking only the best and the most fit of his warriors. The rest were either assigned to the protection of the hold or were herding his villagers into the mountains to

await the outcome. The warriors escorting them
were those he considered to be too old or in-
capacitated for tomorrow's work. They would
have been all right if the fight was to have been
from the wall of the hold, but it wasn't. He would
need young arms and lungs for the next day's
slaughter. He chose to fight in the field away from
the walls of Helsfjord, because to do otherwise, he
would have had to bring in all his villagers to protect them, and there simply wasn't enough food in
the storerooms to be able to withstand even a short
siege before starvation would set in. He had seen
the results of sieges before and knew the terrible
suffering it would have on the women and children
inside. It would be better this way. At least, those
that died would not have to suffer long. Better a
quick cut than lingering hunger and sickness.

His warriors grumbled when, upon arrival, he
made them take out hoes and shovels from the supply packs. Hoes were for women, not warriors.
With a few quick words in which he threatened to
send back anyone who didn't instantly obey, Casca
silenced their protests—especially when Glam took
one out and at Casca's directions began to dig. The
others quickly followed suit.

As Casca judged it, the Saxons probably
wouldn't attack until they were at least fifty feet
away. That was the maximum distance they would
be able to throw their axes from. They would advance to about two hundred feet, then rush. At fifty feet, would come the first wave of axes, and then
the attack would begin in earnest.

Casca was strict in his instructions to keep the
top layer of grass whole and had his men cut it out
in squares and lay it aside. The trench was only to

be about thigh-deep, dug in a straight line across the field with the ends going up along the sides of the tree line to form an open-ended box. If the Saxons tried to flank them by attacking through the trees, they would have to cross his small trench first. Inside the trench, he had sharpened stakes placed and then branches were gathered to interlace over the top. The squares of grass-covered sod were then placed on top of this and carefully arranged to give no hint that there was anything but solid ground beneath. His warriors, once they understood the idea, worked even harder to make sure everything would be right. Casca moved back out to the front and looked over their handiwork, making a change here and there until from a distance of twenty feet, it was impossible to detect his trap. It was on this that they would win or lose.

By nightfall, all was ready. He sent scouts out to keep him informed of the enemy advance, and ordered the rest of his men to settle in for the night. They were permitted to build campfires. This night he wanted it to be no secret where they were. With the Saxon forces outnumbering him by at least five to one, he felt confident they wouldn't hesitate in their advance.

Later that night his scouts informed him that the Saxons had also made camp and were no more than five miles distant.

Casca conferred with Glam and they both agreed that it would probably be at least midday before the Saxons reached their positions. Glam was, as always, ready for whatever would come. He honed down the edge of his sword and axe, stuffed half a lamb down his gullet, and went to sleep, snoring and wheezing. One thing about Glam—

that old bastard didn't seem to have a conscience or a worry about anything. Nothing ever interfered with his eating or sleeping unless it was a quick roll with some sweet young maiden who wanted an experience to remember by coupling with a human bear.

The day broke clear and sharp, ground fog hugging the low spots and hiding in the hollows of the valleys. Before long, it would burn off, leaving the field clear for this day's bloody work. Casca rose with the sun and dressed.

One thing he had learned a long time ago—don't make yourself stand out. Men who affected fancy dress or even armor that was too different from the mass of the men, suffered higher casualty rates. They became selected targets and he had no desire to have a dozen axes and spears coming his way at one time. No, he was a barbarian with the conical helmet with horns. True, he wore his breastplate, but kept it well-hidden under a tunic of gray wolf skin. He kept his short sword in its scabbard for now. A broad-bladed axe, like the one he had killed Ragnar with, would be of more use this day in battering through the wicker shields of the Saxons. He called his captains to him after they had eaten their morning ration of meat and grain.

To Glam he assigned command of the right flank with orders to hold there for his signal unless he saw the center, which he would command, breaking. The left he gave to the proud young warrior, Sifrit, who looked the part of a Nordic hero, blond shoulder-length hair and eyes the color of high mountain lakes. His face was unscarred by battle, not because he had avoided fights but because he was good enough that he won them before he got all cut up. The young man wasted no time on theatrics. When it came to killing, he was all business.

Casca wished he might have had a few of the engines of war that were standard issue in the legions; even a couple of arbalests would have been a comfort. Old Corio could have built them. But his rough crew was not ready to handle such sophisticated weapons of destruction. It would be all he could do to keep them in their positions long enough for the Saxons to fall into his trap. It was probably best, after all, to arm them with the weapons they were most familiar with. He felt he was lucky that he had managed to get a dozen of his young men to take up the use of the bow. Most of the tribes of Germania disdained the use of it, claiming the sword, spear, and axe were the only weapons for a man. That type of thinking had cost them more than one battle. Honor is a fine thing so long as it doesn't get you killed.

He called over the two teenage warriors he had selected as his trumpeters. They only knew three calls: a long blast on the ox horn, two short blasts, and three short blasts. Casca had remarked more than once to Glam that communications were more often than not the secret to success in battle. The leader that could get his orders to his troops the fastest had the best chance of success. If only man had some way to communicate instantly with his forces . . . but that was likely never to be.

The field was silent. Small animals had taken to their borrows; the larger ones had fled far away. Even the birds were silent, staying in the branches of the trees or in their nests. They knew somehow that violence would soon break the silence. Casca often wondered how the dumb beasts could anticipate the actions of man. But they knew. More than once the sound of silence had warned him of an enemy's approach.

And it would be soon now. The last of the scouts were racing across the field. The Saxons wouldn't be far behind. One of the scouts leaped over the camouflaged trench and saluted Casca. "They come, lord. Led by Hrolthar Bluetooth."

Casca laughed at the name. Bluetooth. These Nordics took things literally and named themselves so. Hrolthar did indeed have a tooth that had died and turned dark in color, sitting right in the front of his mouth.

Glam whistled and pointed with his long sword to the far edge. The leading elements of the Saxons were coming out of the trees, first one, then another. They were big hard men with the look of those who enjoyed slaughter. Most, like his own men, had only bare skin for armor. They were a little fairer in color than his own men and more of them were blond or red-headed. All affected beards or long sweeping mustaches that reached below their chins. Only the young men who did not have enough years to grow face hair were clean-chinned.

Casca had wanted his men to shave, but an order like that could have caused rebellion, even after he'd explained how handy a beard was for an enemy to grab onto and hold a man down while he beat his brains out. But it was no use—they had such an affection for hair on the face that it was best to leave it alone. Maybe he could do something about it later with the younger men. Right now they could have their way. It was worse to give an order you couldn't enforce than not to give one at all.

Glam and the other captains had smiled in anticipation as they understood the reason for Casca ordering the women to make up large wicker shields. They were large enough to cover two men, but light enough for one to hold. They made sure their men also understood the use of them and would wait for the command. And the time would be soon.

Chapter Thirteen

Casca called out to pass the word to get ready. The five-foot-tall wicker shields were laid facedown in front of the first rank. He had only two ranks. The men in the rear were all armed with lances and boar spears to protect the first, who would have their hands full soon enough.

Glam, on the right, signaled his readiness, as did Sifrit on the left. Casca looked carefully at the faces of those who were in battle for the first time. They were bright faces of young men, unscarred and handsome. He knew what they were feeling, what caused the slight tremor of the sword arm, the sudden small beads of sweat on the upper lip and brow.

He knew well the feelings that always come before a fight, but they would pass. With the first thrown spear or axe, they would pass, and these young men would do good service this day as young men have always done in their first fights when well-led and not uselessly sacrificed. He knew too that many of these clean, bright faces would be gashed, bloody, and still before the next hour passed. That was the sadness of war. These young men would never sire sons to carry on. All they

would leave behind would be their fathers and
mothers to mourn for them. But he also knew they
would not have it any other way. To be left out of
the fight was worse than the threat of death. How
many millions had died in the name of some honor
that would soon be forgotten in a few years? But
without honor, what else did man have to distin-
guish him from the beasts? Bad as honor could be,
it would be worse to have none.

The Saxons were setting up their ranks. There
was no sense or order to them, just a thick mass of
men on the far side of the clearing, waiting for the
word to attack. Then they would rush. A large warrior stepped forth and bellowed across the field, "Is
the Roman with you, or has he fled back to the
pigpens that sired him?" Casca stepped out a bit
from the straight line of his rank. "I'm here."

Casca knew the Saxons had been marching since
dawn; it would be best if he could get them to attack now, before they had a chance to rest.

"Is that Hrolthar Bluetooth trying to speak like
a man? Aye, it must be, though I'm too far away to
see your rotten tooth. The stench of decay that
reaches me must be coming from your mouth. If
you have the nerve to come a little closer to me, I'll
close that cesspool forever."

Hrolthar stamped his leather-wrapped feet in anger.

Casca grinned to himself. *That got his ass a little
bit.*

Hrolthar called back, "I'll come soon enough,
Roman, but first I have a little entertainment for
you."

Hrolthar signaled, and the mass of his men
opened to let eight of Casca's villagers be shoved

out to the forefront. Obviously, they were all from the same household and had been too late in leaving. There were two old men, a teenage boy and girl, a farmer, his wife, and two small children holding onto their mother's skirt. At a given signal, all eight were cut down, even the children, who were tossed in the air on spear points, while their parents were hacked into pieces by swords and axes. Casca's men groaned in anguish. Many started to break ranks and rush across the field. Only his immediate and firm order to hold stopped them, but it was an unwilling obedience. He called to his men.

"That's what they want you to do, to come to them where they can use their numbers to swarm over you. Stay in line a bit longer and you'll have all the revenge you will ever need; they will come to us. But remember what you have just seen. There will be no mercy asked for or given this day. Kill or be killed."

Casca called back to Hrolthar. "I see the stories are true. You are indeed a man to be feared, especially if one is a woman or child. But if you have the stomach for facing a man, then come to me. We are less in number than you. Surely you have some courage left after your bloody victory over the children. Come then, you bag of pig gut, or all will know you are less than a man, less even than the worms that feed on dead man's eyes; for you are a coward. . . ."

Hrolthar fumed, his face turning red. He beat his chest with his axe hand, his mustache flaring, eyes red-rimmed with the building of the berserker rage. He worked himself up and the contamination spread to his men. They beat on their shields and howled like beasts of the forest, their faces red, sweaty eyes narrowed. They crowded together, feeding each other's battle frenzy.

Casca could feel the moment building. It wouldn't be long now; they were just about ready.

The screaming of the Saxons reached a crescendo that broke in mid-howl and they lunged forward, a disorganized mob racing to the waiting line. Casca moved back into the ranks, beside his trumpeters, to get ready. The Saxons were almost to the point of no return. Those in front of the racing pack had their throwing axes out, one in each hand. Wild-eyed and screaming, they came to a distance of thirty feet and then all of them drew back their arms to throw the deadly flying blades into the line of Casca's warriors.

Casca barked at his trumpeters, "Now!"

They raised their horns and blew one long blast. Now the real use of the wicker shields was made known. The front rank raised them up and knelt behind them, covering themselves and the men behind, who pointed their spears out past the front of their shields to hold off any Saxons who might break through the trench. Axes thudded into the wicker. A half dozen of Casca's men fell to the ground mortally wounded or dead because they hadn't gotten their shields up fast enough. But the brunt of the axe attack was absorbed by the wicker shields.

Immediately behind the throwers came the rest of the Saxons. By the sheer force of their numbers, they forced their brothers in the front into the trap. When they hit the hidden pits their eyes went wide, as the ground that had looked so solid a moment before broke beneath their feet and sharpened stakes penetrated their legs and stomachs. A hundred Saxons died in that first rush onto the trench. Those behind didn't hesitate a moment. They used the bodies of their dead comrades as bridges to cross the gap, only to meet the large shield of wicker that was forming a solid wall forcing them back into the pits. The second ranks' spears darted and stabbed. The young warriors of the center were doing their job. For a moment the Saxon line wavered.

Casca knew the signs. He had seen them often enough when fighting with the Seventh Legion on the other side of the Rhine. Now was the moment. He called to his trumpeters again. Two short blasts were sounded over the din of the battle. The wings of the left and right flanks, those with the older, more experienced warriors under the leadership of Glam and Sifrit, rushed forth using the wicker shields as foot paths over the sharpened stakes. They rushed, axes swinging, the thirst for revenge driving them on. Men fell by the dozens, disemboweled and dying, as the men of the hold paid back a blood debt. The Saxon flanks were crushed and Glam's warriors joined with those of Sifrit in closing the pocket.

The Saxons turned to flee, only to find every possible way out blocked by grim-faced men with spears and axes. The numbers were about equal now, but the spirit of the Saxons was diminished by the unexpected turn of events. Instead of an easy victory over their outnumbered opponents, they had lost half their men in ten minutes. They huddled together, back to back, weapons facing out in a circle inside the pocket. They had nowhere to go. Several threw themselves at the surrounding men only to find their death a little sooner than the others would.

Casca stepped across the trench, using the bodies of dead Saxons instead of the wicker bridges. Hrolthar watched him. Casca signaled again, and the trumpets blew three blasts. His men stopped fighting and pulled back a little. The field was silent again except for the labored breathing of the fighters and the groans of the dying or wounded.

Casca called to the Saxon chieftain, "Are you ready to face me now, baby killer?" Hrolthar waved his axe at the Roman. "You wanted me to come to you earlier. Now if you want me, come to us. We will take many of you with us before this day's bloody work is done."

Casca knew he spoke the truth. When men are surrounded with no way out and no hope for surrender, they have only one choice—to fight to the death and take as many with them as they can. Casca called out to Glam, "Show them the way out."

Glam obeyed and his men stepped back, leaving a corridor to the tree line. It was a corridor lined with steel, but still it represented the only choice other than certain death. Casca pointed. "There is your way out." He knew many would probably escape, but that was better than having too many of his own killed just for revenge. Besides, the survivors would tell their tale and in the telling, the story would grow. Then perhaps fewer would dare to attack the Roman and his men in the future.

"Saxons, there is your way home. Take it or die where you stand." He raised his short sword above his head and cried out, *"Attack!"* His young men dropped their shields of wicker and drew swords and axes. They closed in on the Saxons; only the way out was uncontested. The Saxons made their decision and rushed for the corridor, stomping each other as many fell to the ground in their haste to get away. Glam's and Sifrit's men did bloody duty, with little loss to themselves as they cut down any that came too close to the wall of steel.

Casca lunged forward, grabbed Hrolthar's shoulder, and swung him around, making a sweep with his short sword. It sliced through Hrolthar's right arm at the wrist, dropping the hand still holding the axe to the ground. Hrolthar screamed and before Casca could cover his eyes, Hrolthar used the fountain of Tyr to blind him. For a moment the red, spouting arterial blood from the severed wrist covered Casca's eyes. He reeled back and by the time he had wiped them clear, Hrolthar was gone, holding his wrist tightly with the other hand. He had made his way through the corridor to the tree line and escaped into the woods.

But most of Hrolthar's men had no such degree of fortune and lay gape-mouthed with vacant eyes, waiting for the ravens to pick them clean. In the end, only fifty-four Saxons returned to their homes. The rest were now no more than fertilizer for the field of Runes. No prisoners were taken. All wounded Saxons were put to the sword. It was a hard life and compassion was not a survival factor in these lands. . . .

Casca only regretted that he wasn't able to finish off Hrolthar. But one thing was for certain: the bastard would never use an axe with that hand again. He kicked the severed limb into the ditch to lie there with the dead Saxons until the rest of the casualties had been thrown into the pits and the trenches covered over.

Casca led his men back to the hold carrying with them the spoils of their victory. There were shields, weapons, some bracelets of hammered copper and silver, and a few scraps of bloody armor.

They also returned with their own dead. Carrying them on shields, held high on their shoulders, they returned their own fallen heroes to their families.

Lida stood on the ramparts facing inland, sightless eyes staring in the direction from which she knew they must come. Her ears, grown more sensitive since her blindness, had heard the thin distant sounds of metal striking metal before the waiting guards caught sight of anything with eyes. She called out below to the courtyard. "He comes! Casca is returning!" Somehow she knew that it would be him and not the Saxons that would come to Helsfjord this day.

Chapter Fourteen

The years that followed the battle of the field of Runes was, for the most part, quiet. There were a few more skirmishes with wandering bands of raiders, but the word went far that the pickings at Helsfjord were not worth the trouble it would take to get them.

Casca's young men grew into full-fledged warriors, and they took to the new discipline that he introduced, though not to the degree that the more civilized regions of the world had submitted to regimentation. But they had taken to it still more than any others in their parts. And it served them in good stead when, time and again where they were less in number, they'd won because of the basic obedience they'd given to Casca's orders. The wild blood for battle was still in their breasts, but the history of victory they had achieved made it plain to the most unruly that Casca was right in what he wanted from them, even if it went against their grain. They would obey.

They knew now that there was something strange about their foreign lord, and Glam had explained it in terms they could understand. Casca was one touched by the gods to walk the earth, and by that name, he became known throughout the northlands as "Casca the Walker." They had also made one blood oath to him. They knew that to disobey or break their oath would bring his full anger upon them, and not even the ones who had the touch of berserker about them wanted to face him in his full wrath.

That oath, sworn on the heads of their children, was to never reveal to the Lady Lida that Casca did not age, that he was as he would always be. And this oath was kept by all—not only out of fear of him but out of love for the blind "lady of the hold." They had in their hearts a noble sensitivity that loved a good tale and legend and knew that they were participating in one of the moments of magic the bards sang of. Some of their songs would be of Casca and Lida. They were the hold's secret, and jealously guarded against outsiders. As their lord protected them, so they would die to keep pain away from his lady and kill any who attempted to speak to her of Casca's condition and curse. And indeed, several strangers that heard vague stories of the strange master of Helsfjord found their tongues silenced forever when they visited the domain of "the walker" and let their tongues wag too much in the taverns.

As for Casca, his was the best life he had ever known. Sometimes he could forget for weeks what he was and just be a doting husband. He enjoyed the hours he could spend with Lida, walking with her in the spring through the fields and valleys while being her eyes. Telling all that he saw was a pleasure he didn't willingly share. And she taught him the meaning of strong gentleness. Their only sorrow was that there were no children. Casca

wasn't sure, but perhaps that was best. Though
Lida wanted his child, he was sure it would never
happen. He often wondered if a child of his would
inherit his sickness. That was too great a burden to
put on anyone.

But Lida never complained. There were the children of the hold for her to care for, and they knew
that if they needed anything they were always welcome at the home of Lida. Indeed, it was not uncommon on the nights when the storms came and
the thunder and lightning rumbled through the
stone walls for Casca and Lida to feel one or two
small bodies climbing into their bed and snuggling
close to the lady and master for comfort. These
were the children whose fathers and mothers had
died. They were the children of the hold and would
never know the want or the lack of love. There
would be no beggars in the land Casca ruled, no
children slaves. In his house, they would grow
strong and not be cast out as were the orphans of
Rome and the civilized world. Those outcasts were
destined to roam the streets and alleys or be sold as
slaves to the highest bidder, becoming the play-
things of perverts and deviates who would con-
taminate them with their own sickness of spirit. In
Helsfjord, they would grow as normal men and
women. These were the children of Casca and
Lida, and they were loved as such. Still, it was a
little irritating on those nights when Casca and
Lida wanted to make love to have to stop because
of a small voice saying "I'm scared." But it was a
small price to pay for the pleasure they gave Casca
and Lida as they watched them grow and learn.

Casca's beard grew longer, as did his hair, until
he looked the part of a barbarian chieftain. If he

was to live among these people and rule them, it was best that he looked the part. The beard served to conceal the fact that his face did not wrinkle with the passing of years, though Lida often remarked on what good condition he kept his body in.

Winters came and passed and the young children became men and women and were replaced by others as they went to form their own households. Forty years of love and sharing went with the seasons, and each was better than the last. The fact that Lida was nearing sixty did nothing to lessen her beauty in his eyes and he took no other woman. To him, she was as ageless as he. And she still had the figure of a young girl and a mind as sharp as a Roman senator. She was beautiful, and even at her age she brought forth sighs from young warriors who admired her and even envied Casca his wife.

One thing did eat at him as the years passed, and that was the knowledge that one day she would leave him and he would be alone again, even more than ever before. And he wondered if even centuries could ever fill the void he knew there would be when she left him. This thought bothered him more than anything else. . . . When she left, he would be alone. . . .

Casca stood on the beach on rocks smoothed down by centuries of washing waves that came and went. He looked out to the deep waters and wondered what lay beyond. Several fishing boats were heading out to the open sea to hunt for seal or to spread their nets for fish. They were long, shallow boats that were easy to handle. He wondered how these same boats would do if he could have a couple made a little larger and rigged them with a sin-

gle bank of oars. The shallow draft of the boats
would enable them to go almost anywhere, and if
they were large enough they would probably do all
right in the open sea. He made a mental note to
question Corio about combining some of the features of the galley with those of the shallow fishing
boats.

His meditation was interrupted by the druid.
Casca didn't like the man much and knew he had
been trying to stir up trouble for him among the
villagers, claiming that Casca was a usurper and
had no rights to the hold and the domains of
Ragnar. The old bastard tried his best to carry off
the image of a man of great wisdom and magical
powers. Casca knew he was a phony and was only
feeding his own ego, but others did believe in him
and the fortunes he cast. Lately, he had been fore-
casting doom and misery in several assorted varie-
ties if they didn't get rid of the Roman.

The priest was still pissed off because Casca had
stopped him from making the spring sacrifice to
Mother Earth with the blood of a young virgin
slave girl and boy. The fact that spring had come
and the fields had yielded a good harvest in spite of
their not being fertilized by innocent blood had really ticked off the old bastard.

Carrying his staff of oak, Hagdrall made his way
over the slick stones, slipping a couple of times and
almost busting his sacred fanny on the rocks.

A little disgruntled at the interruption, Casca
spoke to him. "Well, what the Hades is it now, you
phony son of a bitch?"

Hagdrall drew himself erect, his eyes flashing
over his large hooked nose. He waved his staff at
the Roman. "Have care. It is not wise to speak

with disrespect to the representatives of the gods. They could strike you dead for such insolence."

Casca laughed. "That's one thing I'd like to see them do. Now, what is it? Can't you find anything more to bitch about?"

Hagdrall was furious. He was used to having his own way. Even with old Ragnar, he usually got what he wanted. But this foreigner refused to show him any respect. Pointing his staff straight in Casca's face, he said, "You have not heard the last from me. Your troubles are just beginning. Before I'm through with you, you will go on your knees and beg the forgiveness of myself and the gods."

Casca slapped the staff away from his face and grabbed Hagdrall by his gray beard, bringing tears of pain to the old fraud's already watery eyes. "Now you listen to me. If you open that gap-toothed mouth of yours once more, I'll take that staff of yours and ram it so far up your ass, it'll push your tongue out far enough to kiss your butt." Casca gave the beard a jerk and sent the priest to his knees.

Hagdrall continued to curse between pain-clenched teeth. "I have powers, spells to strike you with."

Casca had had just about enough. "Powers? You old faker, I'll show you some power." Releasing the old man's beard, he drew his sword and put the edge to the druid's throat. "The magic *I* have is such that with one easy movement of my wrist your head will lie on the stones and no power on earth could put it back where it belongs."

The druid began to whimper. "Mercy, lord! I meant no harm. I am just an old man whose mind wanders at times. Mercy, lord."

Casca gave the blade a delicate twist and cut a thin mark across the druid's throat. "If your mind wanders, priest, then I would suggest that your body do likewise while it still can. If you're still within our borders by dawn I'll personally feed you to the sea crabs for breakfast."

Hagdrall swore to do as Casca ordered, anything . . . if he would only remove the sword from his throat. Casca let the old man go and made his way back up the path to the hold.

That night he entertained several of his chiefs of the village and they talked over their plans for the coming winter. The details of administration had always been enough to send him packing; only Lida's being there to guide him got him through the process. She had a mind that forgot nothing. Not even the smallest detail escaped her attention. Tactfully, she would whisper the proper answers to Casca when he had to make decisions on matters he was unfamiliar with; the chiefs usually left well-satisfied that justice had been done.

This night was no different from any of the others they'd spent since he'd become lord. Lida sat on his right, the spot usually reserved for visiting nobles. The left was reserved for Glam, and next to him, Sifrit, who had long since become a good and loyal friend to Casca.

Hagdrall sat at his customary place next to the mistress of the household, careful to avoid the gaze of Casca. After the duties of rule were dispensed with, they settled down to eating and feasting as only the men of the north can do. Great platters of roasted meats were set before them and the trenchermen attacked them with gusto. The horns and cups were kept filled with beer, mead, and wine. Toasts were made and given back time and time again. Almost anything served as reason enough to empty and fill the cups; around the table they took turns wishing the lord and his lady and themselves good fortune and happiness. Even old Hagdrall put a smile on his shriveled face and, reaching over, filled cups for Casca and Lida. Casca, already half-stoned from the various brews he'd consumed, paid little attention when Hagdrall sat the fresh-filled cup of honeyed mead before him.

Rising, the druid hoisted his cup and called upon the elemental spirits of the earth and sun to protect all in this place of friendship. Casca raised the cup given to him by the druid, but before he could set it to his lips, Lida whispered firmly, "Stop!"

Reaching out a hand, she found his arm and traced it down to the cup he held. Taking it from him, she held it close to her face and breathed in. Moving her other hand, she grabbed the sleeve of the druid and placed the cup in his hand. "Drink."

Casca watched with growing awareness. Lida was blind, but she'd learned other skills to replace that of sight. Her hearing and senses of touch and smell were three times as keen as any seeing person's, and she could read the truth in a voice, as well as the lies. Behind the softness of her words there lay raw steel. "Drink, druid."

Casca rose from the table to give added strength to her words. The old druid's hand trembled, threatening to spill the contents of the cup meant for Casca.

The Roman spoke softly. "Don't spill it, priest. It could save you a lot of pain. Remember the sea crabs? They'll be waiting for you in the morning if you don't drink."

Hagdrall steadied himself. He knew that Casca meant what he said and that at least the cup offered him a quick death. He had heard the screams of those tied to the tidal stakes too many times to have any illusions about what awaited him. He raised the cup and swallowed it all in one draught.

"There, it's done, Roman pig." Hatred filled his voice. "Curse you and yours. I curse you until the end of time."

Casca grinned, "You're a little late for that, old man. It's already been done, but nice try anyway."

Hagdrall slumped forward over the table. Casca prodded the body with his finger. "Well, whatever it was that he drank, it sure works damn fast."

He motioned for Glam to clear the old man's carcass off the table so that the feasting could continue. The silence around the Hall was broken by a laugh from Glam, and the rest of them joined in. Being good-natured sports, they appreciated a good joke and the one that Lady Lida had put over on the druid had been, "By Mjolnir," a good one. And besides, they hadn't really liked the old priest that much anyway.

Chapter Fifteen

When old Corio took the time off from building the ships Casca wanted, he would be teacher to the children of the hold. He was very patient with them and thoroughly enjoyed this task. In turn, the children grew to love and respect him. Corio would sit on the steps of the hold and try to press some knowledge into the heads of the children. It was hard going; the boys only wanted to hear of battles and glory. The fine art of mathematics was to them something they could see little use for. But they were ordered to attend the classes by the lord and as good little warriors they obeyed, if some what reluctantly. They made their marks on thin sheets of parchment from which the thin ink could easily be washed off and the parchment used over and over again. In spite of their inclinations, a few of them actually did learn to add and subtract.

For Corio it was a good life, although he sometimes missed the luxuries one could find in the boundaries of the empire. Certain foods he had had a fondness for he especially missed—oysters in clam sauce and some fish that could only be found in the warmer waters of the Mediterranean . . . and the wine. He sighed wistfully at the thought of how good a long draught of a cup of rich red Falernian would taste. Here he had to do with thin beer and mead. True, there was an occasional day when some of the scarce wine in the cellars of the hold would be brought out to celebrate some occasion or other. But those days were all too seldom.

Corio scratched his bald pate and leaned back to take his ease in the thin sunlight while the children did their lessons. This was the time when he could let his mind flow and thank the gods for the day when Casca found and bought him and then set him free. He had in turn tried to do as much as he could to make the confines of the hold more tolerable.

His greatest achievement was the toilet he had built, which used rainwater collected in cisterns on the roofs to wash away the human waste. To the villagers of the region this was an unheard-of luxury; on any given day you could find a number of them lined up outside the one he had built for general usage patiently waiting their turn to use the device. Corio knew that many of them didn't really have to go; they just liked to listen to the sound of the water flushing in the crapper. That and the baths were his proudest accomplishments. True, they did not equal the bathhouses of imperial Rome, but they did serve to relax and cleanse the body. And after the lord of the hold had set the example, there were even several of his warriors that had tried the hot soaks themselves, although they had been warned by their friends that washing off their outer layer of dirt would leave them more susceptible to sickness and bad health. It was also well-known that a good coating of grease and ash helped keep the body warmer in winter.

Lately Corio had been eyeing the shallow boats the northmen used for fishing and trading, thinking about how much more graceful they were riding in the wind than the cumbersome lumbering galleys of the empire. Their only fault was that they were of little use in the open sea and were confined to the rocky coasts, never going out of sight of land. But the design was sound; if there was just some way he could figure out how to combine some of the strength of the galleys with the handling capabilities of the long boats.

Often he and Casca had sat watching the sea otters off the rocky beaches, lying on their backs in the kelp beds or twisting and sliding their way into the waves. The sea otters didn't fight the water—they twisted their way through it. If only he could figure out how to make a ship do the same thing. Perhaps there was a way in which the planks could be joined that would give them at least some of the flexibility of the otters, even if the movement was only slight. In a ship like that a man could sail to where the oceans themselves dropped off the rim of the world into the abyss. Twisting? He must give that some more thought; perhaps a way could be found.

He roused himself from his reverie and returned his attention to his charges. He gave them only a halfhearted quiz on their lesson and then dismissed them. They went running off to the sea to gather crabs.

Crabs! He gave a shiver. He had heard about Casca being staked in the tidal pool for the crabs to feed on. It gave him a queasy feeling every time he ate one of the things.

Corio went back inside to find Casca sitting by

Lida playing with some of the children in the Great Hall. Corio excused himself to Lida and took Casca off to the side to discuss the idea of building some completely new ships with some form of interlocking planks that would give them a tiny portion of the flexibility of the sea otters. Casca agreed and told Corio that he could start on the project the following spring. But he could give the orders now for a detail to cut trees and set them out to be cured so they would be seasoned when the time came for them to be used in laying the keels and decking.

Corio left Casca to Lida and the children and on his way back to his quarters he passed Glam heading out to do what he called a little raping and ravaging in the village below. He claimed it helped in clearing up the zits. Corio sometimes worried about Glam. He never knew how to take the bearish hulk. Glam would sometimes affect the most outlandish postures and you could never tell for sure if he was serious. One such example was that Glam considered himself to be an accomplished songwriter and poet, but what he claimed to be one of his best works was a filthy little ditty he titled "You Broke My Heart Then I Broke Your Jaw." Glam continued on his way and left a baffled Corio behind to return to his own spartan quarters where he began working out the design problems of his new ships.

Glam, on the other hand, was having problems of his own. His latest paramour was trying her best to get him married and he wasn't having any of it, so she had cut him off. Sulking over his lack of ability to change the lady's mind, he did his usual number and got blind staggering drunk and wrecked the tavern. It took seven of Casca's largest warriors to haul him off when they responded to the call for help from the terrified innkeeper.

Glam was properly remorseful the next day for the outrages he had performed on the hapless innkeeper, and his three serving wenches who were so sore that they wouldn't be able to serve anyone else for at least two days. However, no one could say that Glam wasn't a fair man and he made proper restitution by presenting the innkeeper with two kegs of wine and one of beer, which of course he borrowed from the hold's cellars. He helped his throbbing head by draining off at least a quarter of another keg. Burping, he made a mental note to tell Casca to put the stuff on his bill. But, as he knew, he was dreadfully absentminded and would probably forget before nightfall. But then, it was the thought that counted, wasn't it?

Glam stumbled his way upstairs to the main hall from the cellars to see if he could get anything to eat when he met Sifrit and conned him into going back into the village with him for another round. He complained all the way about his latest ladylove's lack of understanding and compassion for a high-spirited eagle such as himself.

Sifrit liked the hulk, but personally thought that Glam was carrying things a little too far and thought at his age that he should start to settle down and leave the hell-raising to the younger men. Glam snorted so hard when Sifrit suggested this that he almost sucked his mustache up his own nostrils when he inhaled his next breath.

"Sifrit, I am wounded that you would even think of making such an observation. Leave it to the younger men indeed! Why, the mewling things barely can figure out how to mount a dead horse, much less a lively wench. No! It is my duty to set an example for the young to follow and emulate. Not that any of them could ever come close to matching my abilities with wenches or the bottle. But still, the darling little boys have to have some goals in life, don't they?"

Sifrit sighed deeply. There was no way to get through that bony mass that served Glam for a head and reach his brain with any kind of logic. Sifrit decided that he would just have to play dirty. After all, it was for Glam's own good. The bear was bound to kill himself one day if he wasn't taken in by a firm hand. Sifrit smiled to himself as he helped Glam down a gallon of mead in record time. And he knew just the person to do it. Poor Glam.

Chapter Sixteen

All this time, Glam had been happy for Casca and Lida, but still, he missed not having the free life and the togetherness that they had given up with Casca's marriage, although, he felt he personally had not forfeited as much as Casca. He still haunted the taverns and countryside, hopping into the sack, a pile of hay, or a grassy field with every willing—and some not so willing—maiden. No! By Thor's great hammer Mjolnir, the married life was not for him! It would be a crime to deprive the women of the world of their greatest experience, and selfish beyond reason to restrict himself to just one female when he could satisfy the dreams of dozens.

No! By the holy Aesir, it was his duty to spread his seed among the tribes and improve the bloodlines of the race. And Glam was not a selfish man.

Farmers took to locking up their daughters, wives, and maiden aunts when word got out that Glam was in the region.

It was commonly believed that if Glam's head were ever split open to expose his innards, there would be no brain there—only one giant, female sexual organ. For surely that was all he ever seemed to have on his mind.

While on the prowl, Glam had caught sight of a sweet young thing with hair long enough to drown in and thighs that looked strong enough to crack the ribs of a horse. Whenever he came close or tried to talk to her, she refused to listen to his promises of unequaled pleasure that would fill her nights forever with fond remembrances.

Asking around, he found out that she had come from a neighboring village and was spending the summer with friends of her family. She appeared to be about twenty, well over the age for marriage and, Glam figured, no wonder! For if she had re-fused *his* advances, the girl had to be a little weak-minded. But no matter—he wasn't really interested in how smart she was. He just wanted one night in those strong, well-fleshed arms.

Her continued denial of him began to drive Glam insane. He even went off his feed and lost his appetite. He only picked at his food and never ate more than a leg of lamb at any one sitting, washing it down with a gallon of beer. Casca was worried about him, but Sifrit, who'd become Glam's boon drinking companion and wenching friend, told him not to worry. Everything would be all right; he'd personally see to it.

Glam took to following her about, determined to sample the joys he knew she held if only she wouldn't be so stubborn. He even started bathing more frequently after one of the few times that she'd spoken to him she'd referred to him as having the odor of a goat. It took Sifrit to clue him in that he'd been insulted. Glam personally had always liked the smell of goats.

Sifrit tried to tell him to leave the girl alone and

pursue easier game, that she was too much for him.
Glam paid no heed. It took him the better part of
a week to find out her name: Hemming Danesdot-
ter. He liked the sound of it. To Glam, the more
she denied him, the greater was his desire for her.
In his mind, she was the perfect representation of
Nordic womanhood—almost six feet tall with a
single blond braid that reached almost to her but-
tocks, lovely swaying mounds of pleasure that
rolled and twitched at the same time when she
walked. She had icy lake-blue eyes that he knew he
could melt if she would just let him get near
enough.

Sifrit's efforts to dissuade him from following
her did nothing but increase his determination.
Others paid their attentions to Hemming also, but
not for long. Whenever they called on her, Glam
was always nearby, practicing swings with his two-
handed sword. He severed trees with a single blow
or tossed his twenty-pound axe in the air, catching
and twirling it with one hand as a child would a
twig. From the glint in his eye they chose the better
part of valor; it seldom took more than that to discourage any callers. Once, when trying to be rea-
sonable with a young warrior caller of Hemming's,
he did squeeze the boy's arm a little too hard and
broke the bone in his wrist. But he thought anyone
that delicate would have been no good for her anyway.

Glam asked Lida to put in a good word for him
when he found out that Hemming would be among
the guests at the next feast coming up in a week's
time. She was to be seated next to him.

For the rest of the time prior to the feast, he was
as nervous as a virgin in a whorehouse, especially

after he'd gotten a good look at her coming out of the hut of stones where the villagers went for the steam. When she came out, it was early morning with a light mist hanging over the ground. Her hair was undone and hanging loose in a gold, rippling wave. Her thin, flaxen shift was clinging to her damp body, outlining and emphasizing the shape and size of her breasts, which Glam swore rode like two magnificent ramming prows, jutting out straight and firm. It nearly drove him crazy.

When the night of the feast came, Glam nearly outdid himself. He scrubbed his entire body raw, combed his beard and picked the lice from his hair and, following Lida's advice, even cleaned his fingernails. Hemming was a clean woman and, Lida had informed him, she would probably like a clean man. Glam sighed in frustration at the indignities he had to endure in his preparation; but, he thought, maybe it would be worth it.

All were seated at the feast enjoying the food and drink when Hemming made her entrance. Glam almost swallowed his tongue. Her hair was braided about her forehead and intertwined with wild flowers, and her cheeks had a rosy glow of health. Her dress was finer than any he had ever seen, other than the Lady Lida's. It shimmered and flowed on her body when she walked. Cut simply, the dress was of royal blue, hanging almost to the floor, and a girdle of woven silver thread cinched it at her waist. Glam figured that he could almost reach around her waist with just one of his mutton-sized hands.

Lida whispered to him that she'd heard that the material Hemming was wearing was of pure silk and had come all the way from Rome. Glam

whistled between his teeth. He'd heard of the material before and knew that it was worth its weight in
gold. Glam's desire knew no bounds. This girl was
not only beautiful and desirable; she was also rich.

Sifrit watched with scarcely concealed good humor at his friend's efforts to amuse the girl. Glam
had barely touched his food and drank no more
than nine or ten horns of wine and a few beers.

Casca was really concerned about him. The
night wore on. Bards sang and the minstrels
plucked their instruments and blew on reed flutes.
Hemming sang a song of love from her homelands;
during that, Glam thought he would be unable to
restrain himself. As she sang, she stood in the
flickering lights of the fireplace and torches. Her
body swayed with the words of her song. They
were of love and frustration and dealt with how a
young man, rejected by the object of his adoration,
had finally forced the issue and gone to his ladylove in the night, claiming her against all her protests and, by doing so, had made her love him.

She finished her song and walked with long
strides back to sit by Glam, whom she studiously
ignored.

By Mjolnir, he thought, she's fit to be a queen
herself. She'd even put Freya, the wife of Odin All
Father, to shame. He'd almost chewed his beard in
half and did lose one part of his mustache, but still
she'd refused to speak to him directly.

He was starting to get a little peeved by the time
the party ended, and it wasn't until he'd found out
that she was staying the night in the hold in one of
the guest rooms that he brightened up a little.

So, she liked to sing songs about men who took
what they wanted, did she? Sifrit again addressed

his old friend. "Glam, old horse, believe me. It would be best if you left her alone. I'm telling you this as a friend and companion. That girl's not for the likes of you. Why don't you just have a keg or two of wine and forget her? There are plenty of willing wenches about."

Glam glared back. "Other wenches? Since she's come here I haven't been able to get turned on even once. She's driving me crazy, but," and he slyly winked, "I'll teach her a thing or two before this night's over."

Sifrit merely sighed. "I wouldn't try anything if I were you. You don't know what you're letting yourself in for."

Glam snorted. "I'd risk wrestling a snow giant with one hand for just one hour to teach her what a real man is like."

Sifrit patted him on the shoulder. "Well, you can't say I didn't try. Do what you have to, but remember, I warned you. Whatever happens now is all of your own doing."

When the last of the guests had left or had found places to sleep in the hold, Glam stayed by the hearth and waited, letting the last sounds of life fade from the Hall. When he had tried to talk to Hemming before she'd left for her room, she had only looked at him coldly. In the next moment, she flashed him one quick smile, turned her back, and walked away. It drove him mad. What the hell was she trying to do to him?

Once the Hall was asleep, Glam made his way silently through the corridors and climbed the steps leading to the guest rooms. He tripped once and cursed softly. A man had evidently passed out on the steps, unable to make it to his room. He moved on, as much like a cat as he was capable of, making no more noise than a herd of cattle on the move.

Looking over his shoulder as he reached her door, he made sure there was no one about. He took out a thin, slender-bladed knife and used it to slide between the planks of the door, raising the inner latch until he could open the door wide enough to slide through. It squeaked once when he closed it behind him, causing his heart to skip a beat or two.

The light coming through the open window bathed the form of Hemming lying beneath the coverlets of her bed. Her hair was again undone and lay as a golden wave about her head and shoulders. She moved in her sleep and one bare globular breast winked at him. By Thor's bouncing balls, she's naked! That's a stroke of luck.

Swiftly, he removed his clothing, cursing under his breath when the thongs, holding his leggings about his calves, refused to come undone. Finally he gave up and decided to just leave them on. Creeping forward on his toes, he resembled a not-quite-natural ape. He neared her bed and knelt down, looking at the face of the sleeping woman. There was just a hint of a smile on her face. Was she dreaming of him?

Glam covered her mouth with his hand. "Shhhhhh! I won't hurt you," only to receive a crack across his ear that set his head to ringing. Then teeth bit into his hand and the fight was on.

By the gods, she was strong! They struggled and fought, with her biting and kicking, pulling great gouts of hair from his beard and head, her fingernails digging grooves in the fur hide he called his back.

She fought silently; not a word was spoken as they struggled. His weight atop her, he finally forced her back onto the bed and took another five minutes to maneuver himself between her legs, pinning her so that she couldn't get away.

As gently as he could, he penetrated her. She gave one small gasp of pain as her hymen broke. Glam smiled to himself. *Aha! A virgin. Anyone knows a virgin isn't quite right in the head until she gets a proper laying.*

Glam thrust deep and Hemming's eyes went wide, the whites showing in the dark as he entered her completely. Gradually, the struggle turned to mutual efforts of pleasure, and she moaned, softly at first, then louder. Soon her legs were wrapped about him and they rode the "Beast with Two Backs" until they both dropped off into a deep sleep of satisfied exhaustion. They slept, her head on his arm and one of his huge hands holding her breast.

Glam twitched in his sleep. Something had pricked his neck. He moved in his slumber, trying to get away from the annoying feeling, only to feel the pricking sensation again. One eye opened, then the other, both focusing at the same time.

He looked up at the long length of shiny, sharpened steel to see the face of Sifrit standing over him holding the sword to his neck. He tried to move away from the sharp tip of it, but Sifrit shook his head, looking sad, and pressed the point into his neck a bit deeper.

Glam choked out in confusion, "What the crap is wrong with you, Sifrit? What are you doing here? And take that damned ugly toothpick away from my throat."

Sifrit again shook his head, as if in regret. "Sorry about this, old boy, but I tried to warn you. You just wouldn't listen." Hemming woke, stretched her arms, and sighed deeply. Seeing Sifrit, she said nothing. She just rolled over and went back to sleep.

Repeating himself, Glam hissed, "What the Hades is wrong with you, Sifrit?"

Sifrit twitched his blade a bit, drawing a drop of blood. "We got a problem, Glam. The girl is my first cousin and she's here under my vowed protection. You know the laws concerning the taking of a woman against her wishes, especially a virgin. We have a blood feud here."

"Blood feud," Glam sputtered. "What do you mean? That I took her against her will? Just ask her."

Sifrit called out Hemming's name and she opened her eyes and smiled.

"Good morning, cousin," she yawned.

Sifrit asked her, "Did this animal rape you?"

Hemming touched her hair, putting a stray strand back into place and out of her eyes. Her voice was sweet as honey. "Yes, he did, cousin, and not just once but seven or eight times.

Sifrit whistled between his teeth in admiration. "Well, then," he turned his attention back to Glam. "That about does it, old friend. I am sorry about this, but I don't have any choice in the matter. Honor demands that I run this long piece of cold steel through your neck in order to satisfy my family's honor."

Glam bellowed out, "You wouldn't do that. Now, come on, Sifrit, we've been friends too long for you to act this way. Besides, the girl isn't really hurt. She's been gently used."

Sifrit shook his head in the negative. "Gently used, you say—after seven or eight times? No way. It isn't anything personal, you understand. It's just the law. I'm going to have to kill you now or my family will be dishonored and I can't have that happen."

Glam began to protest loudly, his mind confused. Hemming had rolled over on her side and closed her eyes again, apparently oblivious to anything unusual happening around her.

Casca came in through the open door, followed by Lida. He took one look at the situation and could barely restrain a grin. "What's going on here and what's all the noise about?"

Sifrit informed him of Glam's actions and how his virgin cousin had been repeatedly abused. Hemming smiled her agreement to the tale and took on a wounded expression. She lowered her eyes demurely and wiped away a nonexistent tear.

Glam appealed to Casca and Lida. "Isn't there anything you can do about this, Casca? At least make him take that sword away from my throat and give me a fighting chance."

Casca mused a moment, then asked Lida what the customs and laws of the land had to say about matters like this. They whispered together a moment, and Casca said to Glam, his voice full of regret, "I'm sorry, Glam, but Lida says that Sifrit has every right to kill you and that we can't interfere. You know, I've always made it a policy not to interfere with the local customs. I guess you'll just have to have your throat slit. See you later Sifrit,

Hemming," and he turned to leave.

Glam wailed out, "My lady, surely you can help me."

Lida hesitated. "There is one way."

Glam wailed again, "Anything."

Lida was quiet for a second. "The only way that honor could be satisfied would be for you to marry the girl and become a kinsman to Sifrit."

Hemming smiled shyly and under the cover, stroked Glam's thigh. A light lit up in Glam's mind as the pieces came together. "So that's the way it is. You've trapped me. Some damn fine friends you are."

Sifrit responded in a wounded manner.

"I'm sorry you feel that way about things, Glam. But even if it were true, I'd still have to kill you. I thought that at least if I had to kill you, we could still be friends. But if you're going to act bitchy about it, that's your business. If you don't want to marry her, then I have no choice but to finish you off."

Hemming stroked the inside of his thighs with a long fingernail and Glam gave up. "All right, you've got me. I'll marry her." But he shook a warning finger at Sifrit and Casca. "I know you two set me up and one of these days, I'll get even with you for it."

Casca grinned. "Well, now, that's settled. Let's go down and get something to eat."

Sifrit moved the sword point away from Glam's neck and leaned over and gave him a firm thumping on the shoulder. "Glad to have you in the family, old boy. It may not be as bad as you think." He whispered in Glam's ear, "She's rich and I hear she is also a damned fine cook."

Sifrit left and Glam rose, searching for his trousers. Before he got up off the bed, Hemming stuck her tongue in his ear and whispered, "Next time you'll take your leggings and boots off."

The wedding took place five days later and in the spring of the following year, Hemming gave birth to Glam's firstborn, whom they named Olaf, after her father.

Though Glam continued to grumble about the sword wedding he'd been forced into, he fooled no one. The glint in his eyes when he looked at Hemming or when he watched over Olaf told all the truth, no matter how much he complained.

As for Hemming, she was well-pleased and took to training Glam so that his manners and appearance improved much over the years.

Chapter Seventeen

Lida coughed weakly and wiped away some small flecks of blood from her lips with a clean cloth. Casca watched her with worry playing at the edge of his mind. The damned coughing wouldn't go away. For the last year it had hung on and Lida had grown weaker with each day. At night the coughing was at its worst when in her sleep it came in uncontrollable spasms that wracked her thin body, leaving her a little more weary and tired with each dawn. Every cough was a lance in Casca's heart. He had seen the wasting sickness before. There were some who had recovered from it, and he clung to this thin ray of hope, for it was all he had.

But the hope was fading now that a new winter was coming, and in his heart he knew that she could not last through the cold, gusty winds that came in from the frozen sea. He had tried to talk her into letting him take her south someplace, where the sun never faded. He had heard that warmth and sun were good for those who suffered from the wasting sickness and consuming cough. But Lida refused, her clear, sightless eyes watching him. She knew that the healing sun was too late to do her any good and that if she must die, then she wanted to do it in this place, in the home of her people where she and her man had lived and loved all these years. She was content and worried only about Casca. Her weird had been told and soon the weavers would cut her thread of life. There was no denying the truth.

As of late her biggest complaint was that she had to nag and threaten Casca into making love to her. He thought it would take away from her remaining strength. But she needed him and would not do without the closeness of him. When they loved he was as gentle as was imaginable a man could be. With her he was the most caring and gentle of men, and several times she had to chew him out to keep him from being too gentle with her.

As the leaves began to turn in the forests the day came when she knew that they could take no more pleasure from each other's bodies, although the closeness was still there. It was a closeness now of feelings that transcended mere sex. By just a touch of his hand on her cheek he gave her more love than she had ever dreamed possible. He let no one else tend her. He washed her wasting body and coaxed her into taking tiny sips of broth when she had no appetite. And he too waited. He waited for the cruelest event of his long existence to take place. He wandered through the Hall of the hold, lost to himself, and old Glam would shake his shaggy gray head in sadness.

Glam knew he was witnessing one of the great loves of all time, a love that the bards would sing of for centuries to come. The old barbarian knew that something was taking place that he could only re- motely identify with. True, he loved his woman, but he knew that one day he would join her in the great Hall of Odin. He could not fathom the terrible sadness that his friend felt in being left behind forever. Glam knew that for Casca life was a torment. True, there were times when they knew pleasure and enjoyed the things all men do. But it is not natural for a man to go on and on without cease. Everything in creation must die so the new can be born. Glam stroked his gray beard and walked heavily to his rooms. All must die so that the new can be born . . . *all but Casca.*

Casca sat beside Lida's bed listening to the shallow breathing, holding her hand gently in his own scarred paw. Her skin still had that clear, luminescent quality to it that it had when they'd first met. Her hair was the same pale color of moonlight, and the love he felt was as sharp as a sword in his heart. Another world was dying and he couldn't go with her. Unnoticed tears ran from his eyes to lose themselves in his beard. She was beautiful, as only those few who are blessed with timeless love and grace can be. The rages of time that claimed most had kept their distance from her. Her face was still smooth and unlined and, until the wasting sickness settled on her, she had had the walk and grace of a young girl. But she also had the wisdom of age.

She gave a tremor, and for a moment tightened then released her grip on Casca's hand. She tightened her grip once more, as if to make sure he was still there.

Glam stuck his gray and balding head in the door and looked from Lida to Casca. Then silently he left, leaving them to what he knew would be their last moments together. Casca used his free hand to stroke her hair, feeling its fineness between his own rough fingers.

Lida stirred and took a deep breath, held it for a moment, and then released it slowly.

Her eyelids opened. The milky-clear, sightless orbs moved from left to right, then stopped to face Casca directly. She raised her hand to touch his face, running her finger along the hairline scar. She spoke: "You never did tell me how you received this one." For just a second he could have sworn her eyes focused on him and that she could see. Her voice dropped to an even softer note. "I can see you. You haven't changed. You're still the same as when we married." She smiled gently. "It has been for me the best of all possible existences and I thank you for it. I'm only sorry that I have to leave you now. I can hear others calling me from the distance, and I know that I can't wait much longer."

She took another deeper breath, with the hint of a shudder in it. She raised her head from the pillow. "I love you now and always. We will meet again and again. You can never really lose me, whether in this world or the next. I love you now and I will love you a thousand years from now." She raised her face to him and drew his head to her and kissed him long and sweetly. As a wife and a lover, she kissed him. And in that kiss, she gave him her last breath, which he breathed in and held inside as her body went limp and the spirit left her to join those distant voices that called her.

Casca laid her back on the pillow and rose. She had said, *I love you now and I will love you a thousand years from now.* He had once used those very words in a letter to a woman he'd loved and had to leave.

He rose and went to the window. Dawn was breaking red and gold. Another winter was coming. From the north, high in the clear sky, he saw a flight of wild swans heading to the south, sailing the skies with strong, clean sweeps of their wings. Rising from the woods near the hold, he saw another single, graceful bird rise up to join them. A female! The swan circled over the hold once, made one long, lonely cry, and merged with the flock to disappear in the distance. Casca cried, "Are those the voices that called you?" He stood alone in the beginning light of day. Tears ran in rivers down his face as he looked after the disappearing birds and cried out. The people below in the yard who were waiting, and even those in the nearby village, heard his anguish and knew she was gone. *"Lida-a-a-a . . . a thousand years . . ."*

Page-turning Suspense from
CHARTER BOOKS

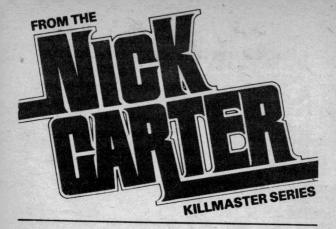

NICK CARTER